spy school GOES NORTH

Also by Stuart Gibbs

The Spy School series

Spy School

Spy Camp

Evil Spy School

Spy Ski School

Spy School Secret Service

Spy School Goes South

Spy School British Invasion

Spy School Revolution

Spy School at Sea

Spy School Project X

With Anjan Sarkar

Spy School
the Graphic Novel

Spy Camp
the Graphic Novel

The FunJungle series

Belly Up

Poached

Big Game

Panda-monium

Lion Down

Tyrannosaurus Wrecks

Bear Bottom

Whale Done

The Moon Base Alpha series

Space Case

Spaced Out

Waste of Space

The Charlie Thorne series

Charlie Thorne and the
Last Equation

Charlie Thorne and the
Lost City

Charlie Thorne and the
Curse of Cleopatra

The Once Upon a Tim series

Once Upon a Tim

The Labyrinth of Doom

The Sea of Terror

The Quest of Danger

The Last Musketeer

STUART GIBBS

spy school GOES NORTH

A spy school NOVEL

Simon & Schuster Books for Young Readers

New York London Toronto Sydney New Delhi

SIMON & SCHUSTER BOOKS FOR YOUNG READERS
An imprint of Simon & Schuster Children's Publishing Division
1230 Avenue of the Americas, New York, New York 10020

For information about special discounts for bulk purchases, please contact Simon & Schuster Special Sales at 1-866-506-1949 or business@simonandschuster.com.
The Simon & Schuster Speakers Bureau can bring authors to your live event.
For more information or to book an event, contact the Simon & Schuster Speakers Bureau at 1-866-248-3049 or visit our website at www.simonspeakers.com.
Interior design by Hilary Zarycky
Endpaper imagery by iStock
The text for this book was set in Adobe Garamond Pro.
Manufactured in the United States of America
0823 BVG
First Edition
10 9 8 7 6 5 4 3 2 1
Library of Congress Cataloging-in-Publication Data
Names: Gibbs, Stuart, 1969– author.
Title: Spy school goes north / Stuart Gibbs.
Description: First edition. | New York : Simon & Schuster Books for Young Readers, [2023] | Series: Spy school ; book 11 | Audience: Ages 8–12. | Audience: Grades 7–9. | Summary: Superspy middle schoolers Ben and Erica must embark on mission to rescue Erica's grandfather, who was abducted from a remote Alaskan training facility.
Identifiers: LCCN 2022049895 (print) | LCCN 2022049896 (ebook) | ISBN 9781665934749 (hardcover) | ISBN 9781665934763 (ebook)
Subjects: CYAC: Spies—Fiction. | Schools—Fiction. | Kidnapping—Fiction. | Rescues—Fiction. | Alaska—Fiction. | Adventure and adventurers—Fiction. | LCGFT: Action and adventure fiction. | Novels.
Classification: LCC PZ7.G339236 Sot 2023 (print) | LCC PZ7.G339236 (ebook) | DDC [Fic]—dc23
LC record available at https://lccn.loc.gov/2022049895
LC ebook record available at https://lccn.loc.gov/2022049896

For Garrett, Simone, Buster, and Bixby

Contents

June 14

From: ██████████████████, Agent Emeritus
To: ███████████████, Head of the CIA
Re: Operation Blazing Phoenix

Dear ███████████████,

The events of this week are a dark moment in the history of the CIA. My beloved alma mater—as well as yours, and that of so many of our other fellow agents—has been exposed and nearly destroyed. There is no way we can safely continue educating students there, meaning that a generation of future agents has been compromised.

But it doesn't have to be a total loss. As you requested, I am enclosing my proposal for espionage training to covertly continue for a select few students who have already proved themselves in the field: ██, and ████████████████████. I volunteer to oversee the continuation of their studies, along with ████████████████ and ██████████ ████████. ████████████████ also volunteered, but I believe he would be a detriment to our students, rather than a boon.)

As this project is to proceed with the utmost secrecy, I would recommend that we relocate to ████████████████████████████████████ and then ███ while also █████████████████████████████████ with ██. Plus, we should absolutely ██████████████████████████████████ or else we'll have a real mess on our hands.

Please get back to me on this immediately. My team is ready to go as soon as you give your word.

Sincerely,

██████████████████

P.S. ████████████████████ was wondering if she could get your husband's recipe for the potato salad he served when we visited you last month. I know it's classified, but you can trust us. We're willing to trade you our recipe for apple cobbler in return.

RELOCATION

Spy School Satellite Facility

Kenai Fjords National Park, Alaska

July 17

1000 hours

Erica Hale dangled from her climbing rope on the cliff face, five hundred feet above the ground, and asked, "What do you smell?"

I paused in the midst of rappelling beside her, quite sure that I hadn't heard the question correctly. "Did you just say, 'What do you smell?'"

"Yes."

I glanced at the ground fifty stories below us and instantly regretted doing so. From that height, even the tallest trees looked as puny as bonsai. Alarmed, I clutched the rock wall so tightly that my knuckles turned white.

Meanwhile, Erica had the calm demeanor of someone sitting on a nice, comfy couch in a room full of throw pillows. "You don't need to hold on to the cliff like that. The friction of your rope in your belay device is strong enough to keep you from falling."

"I know that. But I still feel safer holding on."

"You're *not* safer. All you're going to do is tire yourself out. So let go and relax." Erica kicked off the rock wall and swung out over the void, grinning like a toddler on a playground swing. Her rope groaned under her weight, as though it were thinking about snapping. Erica didn't seem the slightest bit concerned. She pendulumed back to the wall beside me, her boots thudding against the rock.

A few pieces of stone flaked off and dropped down into oblivion below us.

Despite what Erica had just told me, I clutched the wall even tighter. "Could we please head down?"

"Answer the question first."

"What's the holdup down there?" a voice yelled. Forty feet above us, Zoe Zibbell peered over the top of the cliff.

The grinning face of Mike Brezinski appeared beside her. "Is Ben freaking out?"

"No!" I shouted back defensively.

Mike and Zoe shared a knowing look. "He's definitely freaking out," Zoe said.

"Of course I'm freaking out!" I exclaimed. 'We're dangling off a cliff—and instead of rappelling down like normal people, Erica wants to know if I smell anything!"

"The point is to be aware of your surroundings at all times," Erica explained. "Which requires using all of your senses. Right now, you're hyper-focused on the rock in front of you and nothing else."

"The rock is *important*," I explained. "If I fall off of it, I die."

At the top of the cliff, Zoe sniffed the air. "I smell fear."

"That'd be Ben," Erica said.

Which was true. Even though it was summer, it was only fifty degrees in Alaska, plus the windchill. And yet, I was still sweating buckets. I reeked so badly, it was possible that people a mile away could have smelled me.

Mike inhaled deeply. "I smell pine trees," he announced, "with a hint of seawater."

"And a touch of fresh grass," Zoe added. "The fragrance is really delightful."

"It is," Mike agreed. "This whole place is what air freshener is *trying* to smell like."

Although they were perched at the top of an extremely tall cliff, neither of them seemed remotely worried or uneasy.

I was the only one of the four of us with the common sense to be properly terrified about falling to my death. But it was evident that Erica wasn't going to let me descend until I answered her question, which meant that the longer I took, the longer I would spend hanging above the abyss.

Despite my fear, I tentatively sniffed the air. Beyond my own body odor, I picked up on the pine, seawater, and fresh grass that Mike and Zoe had mentioned. And other things as well: the gritty, mineral aroma of the cliff; the hearty, mulch scent of the forest floor . . . and a musty, earthy odor I couldn't quite place. Although something about it seemed important.

So I used my other senses to figure out what it was.

I pulled my gaze from the rock wall and realized that the view from my spot on the cliff was spectacular. It was a rare, cloudless day on the southern coast of Alaska, and I could see for miles in every direction. The mountain I was dangling from was a knob of rock that jutted out of a verdant forest surrounded by a shimmering blue fjord on one side and a jagged range of mountains on the other. The mountains were capped by the colossal Harding Icefield, which was over seven hundred square miles in size and often a mile thick. Numerous glaciers extended from it, snaking down through dark-rock valleys to the water. It was an area so remote and inaccessible that few humans had ever seen it; the mountain my friends and I were on didn't even have a name.

We were completely off the grid. The closest town had only one thousand people and was four hours away by boat—assuming the weather was good. If the weather *wasn't* good (which was often the case), then the closest town wasn't accessible at all. We were staying in a few rustic cabins tucked into the woods on the edge of a glacial lake at the base of the mountain. I could see them below me, although from my height, they looked as small as Monopoly houses. (They were also the same green color as Monopoly houses, so as to blend into the forest.) All our power was solar. Instead of indoor plumbing, we had a latrine. We had brought some dried goods with us to eat, like giant sacks of beans and rice, but for the most part we had been living off plants we foraged and fish that we caught. It was as though we had gone back in time.

Until only a few weeks before, all of us had lived in a very different place: the gothic campus of the CIA's Academy of Espionage in the heart of Washington, DC. For most of its history, the existence of spy school had been a secret. The campus even had an alias: St. Smithen's Science Academy for Boys and Girls. But the school's cover had been blown by a former student turned enemy agent named Murray Hill. Murray was my nemesis. I had thwarted several of his evil plans; in retaliation, he had put a price on my head and leaked the location of the academy to hundreds of assassins. As a result, the CIA had decided the entire training program was compromised, shut it down, and sent all the students back to their normal lives. . . .

With four exceptions.

Erica's grandfather, Cyrus Hale, was a highly respected spy who had proposed a solution to keep at least a fraction of the program going: take a select group of students and spirit us away to an isolated location to continue our training, which Cyrus would oversee personally. The operation was so top secret that only a handful of people at the CIA knew about it. Even our old principal didn't know, although truth be told, our old principal had rarely known anything.

The reason that Erica, Zoe, Mike, and I had been chosen, rather than anyone else, was that each of us had been accidentally field-tested. Normally, students weren't supposed to go on missions until they graduated the academy after seven years of rigorous training—but circumstances had conspired against us. I had only ended up on my first mission through a series of mishaps, when the CIA selected me as bait to catch a mole and Erica had intervened to save me. After that, unusual events had led to Erica and me being on another nine missions together, in which the fate of the world had often hung in the balance. Luckily, we had prevailed.

And so, even though I had only completed a year and a half of spy school—and had just turned fourteen a month earlier—I was one of the chosen few. Zoe and Mike had been selected because they had ended up on several of my later missions. Zoe was also in my year, while Mike was technically a year below us, even though he was our age. (He had been my friend at regular middle school and had only been recruited to spy school after cleverly deducing that it existed.)

Erica was easily the most qualified of all of us. She had completed four years of official training at the academy, but as a member of the Hale family, she had also received unofficial spy training since birth. The Hales had been spying for the United States since before the United States had even existed, and her mother's family had an equally long history of spying for England. So espionage was the family business. (Erica's first sentence had been "You're under arrest for treason.") Because of this, Erica had better spy skills than anyone else at school—as well as most of the adults in the CIA. Which was why she was currently teaching the rest of us, even though she was less than two years older than me.

Erica also happened to be my girlfriend. I had fallen for her hard on my first day of spy school—both literally and metaphorically. She had tackled me in the midst of my first training exercise—and I had been smitten with her ever since. She hadn't been the slightest bit interested in me for quite some time, but over the course of our missions, I had proven to her that I was actually a pretty good spy—and had even helped her become a better spy as well.

Still, I was nowhere near as skilled as Erica was—and probably never would be. Erica had an exceptionally impressive array of talents. To name only a few: She could battle multiple enemy agents in hand-to-hand combat at once, defuse bombs, speak sixteen different languages, drive a car at high speed—and had learned how to fly a helicopter in just the past three weeks. She also had virtually no fear of anything, as evidenced by her relaxed manner as she hung from the cliff face, and her senses were incredibly well tuned. I had seen her detect an enemy by merely catching a whiff of his cologne from a quarter mile away. She had always claimed that such talents were the result of practice, and so, Zoe, Mike, and I had been trying to improve ours over the last few weeks.

It was working. We had been training seven days a week for up to eighteen hours a day, honing espionage skills such as self-defense, decryption, orienteering, and building explosives from standard household items. We had also been doing a great deal of physical conditioning, hauling forty-pound backpacks for miles through the wilderness, swimming across lakes, and ice-climbing glaciers. I could already see a marked difference in all of us. Mike and Zoe had been good athletes when they'd arrived, but now they were like junior Olympians. And even I was in tremendous shape.

I still hadn't become proficient at *everything*, though.

Despite plenty of practice, my weaponry skills remained pathetic. Earlier that day, I had accidentally misfired a crossbow and nearly shishkebabed Cyrus, which he was very displeased about. But in most other areas, I had improved.

Even my senses had gotten better.

As I dangled from the climbing rope, I managed to concentrate and find a sense of calm. I focused on listening to my surroundings and detected—in addition to the rustle of the wind in the trees and the distant lap of the water against the rocky shoreline of the fjord—a faint munching noise well below me. With that, I suddenly grasped what the musky odor I had smelled was.

"There's a bear at the base of this cliff," I informed Erica.

"Yes." She grinned, pleased by my progress. "And what color is it?"

A few weeks earlier, I might have been thrown by this question, wondering how on earth I was possibly expected to tell a bear's color by smelling or hearing it. But now, despite my precarious position on the rock face, I realized I already had all the information I needed.

"It's black," I replied.

We were in one of the few areas of Alaska in which there were no brown bears, like grizzlies, because they had never bothered to migrate across the ice field—and we were too far south to encounter polar bears. Black bears were significantly smaller and less aggressive than grizzlies or polar bears, but you still didn't want to rappel down onto one's head.

Thanks in part to the lack of larger bears in the area, there were *lots* of black bears around our camp. We hadn't done a census, but there were certainly more of them than there were of us, which made late-night trips to the latrine somewhat harrowing. So far, none of us had ever had a bad encounter with one of them. For the most part, they didn't seem to care that we were there, but we still carried bear spray at all times, just in case.

"Correct again," Erica said, in response to my deduction. "So how do we deal with it?"

"We descend slowly, so the bear doesn't think we're a threat. And we ought to make noise, so it knows we're coming and isn't startled."

"Excellent. Luckily for us, it's busy eating a salmon, so it will probably be much more focused on that than you and me, but still, it always makes sense to be cautious."

I gave her a look of surprise. "You can tell what it's eating?"

"I can discern a distinct aroma of dead salmon. Plus, it's a good guess anyhow. Salmon's pretty much all the bears are eating right now."

I nodded, understanding. The salmon had begun returning to the glacial lakes to spawn. Some of the local streams were so thick with them that you could practically walk across their backs. It was like Halloween for bears; their favorite food was everywhere and easy to come by, and they were gorging themselves on it every chance they got.

"Does that mean we can continue down now?" I asked.

"Yes."

I heaved a sigh of relief. "Thank goodness."

During our training, we had experimented with many ways to alert bears that we were nearby. The standard was to simply yell out "Hey, bear!" although that got monotonous on long treks through the wilderness. So we generally had conversations at a much louder tone than usual—or we sang. Erica had turned out to have a gorgeous singing voice and, to my astonishment, an encyclopedic knowledge of Broadway show tunes. She had taught me many over the past few weeks, and I was just about to launch into "The Surrey with the Fringe on Top" as I rappelled down when Erica suddenly tensed beside me.

It was very subtle. Until recently, I might not have even noticed the change in her demeanor. But now I did. "What's wrong?"

"Shhh," she said, then cocked her head slightly, listening.

I listened too. Once again, I heard the happy munching of the bear, but there was something else, even fainter and more distant. It was at the very edge of what I could detect, and yet, when I concentrated, I recognized it as the sound of hand-to-hand combat.

Erica had heard it too. Her eyes went wide in concern. "Grandpa!" she exclaimed, and then began rappelling as fast as she could.

Normally, when you rappelled, you walked slowly down the cliff face in reverse; as the rope passed through the belay device attached to your climbing harness, the resulting friction would prevent you from falling. At first, I had found it unsettling to back down a steep vertical surface, but eventually I had realized it was quite safe as long as you proceeded with care. However, in her haste to get to her grandfather, Erica had thrown caution to the wind. She wasn't rappelling so much as sprinting backward toward the earth; her rope was passing through her belay device so fast that it was smoking.

"What about the bear?" I yelled to her. "Aren't we supposed to be descending slowly so it doesn't think we're a threat?"

"We've got bigger problems than the bear!" Erica yelled back. "Get down here now! All of you!"

"On our way!" Mike shouted from the top of the cliff, and then he and Zoe disappeared from sight. With Erica and me on the climbing ropes, it was faster for them to run down the mountain than to wait for us to reach the bottom and then rappel after us. I could hear their footsteps fading as they sprinted away along the trail by which we had reached the peak.

I warily glanced at the precipitous drop below me. Hurtling down it under normal circumstances would have been scary enough; doing that with a hungry bear at the bottom was absolutely petrifying.

Despite this, Erica was already well over halfway down.

So I gathered my nerve and raced after her.

I didn't descend nearly as swiftly as she did, but I still went much faster than I felt was prudent. I let go of the rope and let it slide through my belay device while I backpedaled down the sheer cliff face. It was sort of like being in an express elevator—without the elevator car. The wind whistled past my ears while the rope sizzled and the forest came rushing up to meet me. It was all rather unsettling—although still much better than a full-on plummet would have been. Before I knew it, I was lowering through the treetops. The landscape grew dimmer as the foliage blocked the sunlight, and I was immediately overwhelmed by the smells of pine, damp moss—and bear.

The black bear I had sensed before was, in fact, not far from where I was about to touch ground, devouring a massive salmon it had hauled out of a nearby stream. It was large for a black bear, at least five hundred pounds by my guess, with claws like meat hooks. Normally, I would have been in no hurry to go anywhere near it. But this was an emergency. Thankfully, the bear was extremely intent on gorging itself, like a cruise ship passenger at an all-you-can-eat buffet, and it was evident that Erica had made it past without any trouble; I could spot her darting through the forest in the distance, heading back to camp, well ahead of me.

I fought every instinct I had about avoiding large, ravenous carnivores and set down on the spongy earth. Despite the bear's presence, I felt a massive surge of relief to be on the ground again. I quickly unclipped my belay device from the rope and did the last thing any survival expert would recommend: I ran full speed toward the bear.

It didn't even look at me. I was sure it knew I was there, though: The hair on its hump stood on end, and it emitted a low, guttural warning growl that I could feel in my bones. And yet, I still wasn't enough of a threat to warrant a break in eating. If I had come much closer, or foolishly tried to take the fish away, the bear would have likely eviscerated me with its claws, but it remained focused on its food as I sprinted past.

I had successfully rappelled down the cliff face and avoided a bear. So I only had whoever had attacked Cyrus to worry about.

Which, now that I thought of it, was certainly the biggest threat of all.

The bad guys, unlike black bears, were obviously looking to cause trouble. It was hard to hear anything over the pounding of my feet and the hammering of my heart, but it seemed to me that the sounds of fighting had stopped. That could have been good news: Cyrus might have defeated whoever had attacked him. Then again, he might have lost, which would be very bad indeed.

It was a quarter mile back to our camp, along a meandering trail that we had hacked through the woods. Thanks to my physical training, I covered the distance quickly. Only a minute after passing the bear, I caught sight of the first cabin.

The camp had originally been built by the US Army during World War II, before Alaska was even a state, back when all the combatants were scrambling to establish military bases around the Pacific. (The Russians and the Japanese had also set up a few outposts in the Alaskan wilderness at that time.) It didn't matter how large each base was; the objective was merely to get footholds on the ground. This particular camp appeared to have been used only rarely since then, and it had possibly been forgotten by everyone in the government except for Cyrus. When we had arrived at the site four weeks earlier, the cabins had been in terrible shape, with leaky roofs, rotting walls, and plenty of uninvited inhabitants. Erica and Zoe had found dozens of voles in theirs, while the one Mike and I shared had a family of wolverines living in it. But we had come with tools, plywood, and wolverine repellent—and some of the original army equipment, like the cast-iron wood-burning stoves, was sturdy enough to withstand a nuclear blast and therefore still operational. So it hadn't been too long before we had everything up and running. Within a few days, the cabins were repaired and downright cozy.

There were eight cabins in total, but we had only refurbished four: one for the girls, one for the boys, one for Cyrus, and one for Erica's parents, Alexander and Catherine Hale, who were currently away on a resupply mission. There was also the latrine and a mess hall (which were thankfully located at opposite ends of the camp from each other), a few equipment sheds, and a drying room for our clothes, which were often sodden, given the generally inclement weather in Alaska. Cyrus had the cabin at the farthest end of camp, closest to the boat dock. He claimed he'd chosen it so he could protect the rest of us from enemy attacks, as those would most likely come from the water—although Erica had told me his real reason was that the cabin was closest to the latrine. (Cyrus's aging bladder wasn't working as well as it used to, and he usually had to get up two or three times a night to relieve himself.)

I slowed as I came through camp, alert for any sign of what had happened in the fight. I didn't see any unconscious enemy agents sprawled on the ground—but I didn't see any sign of Cyrus, either. I cautiously made my way past the mess hall and the other cabins until I arrived at Cyrus's.

Someone had knocked his door off its hinges to gain

entry, most likely the enemy. I paused a few feet away, worried that a few bad guys might still be lurking inside.

I heard footsteps coming toward the doorway. And then Erica raced out, looking as distraught as I'd ever seen her.

"He's gone!" she said. "They took him."

"Who's they?" I asked.

"I don't know, but they couldn't have gone far."

Behind Erica, I caught a glimpse through the open doorway of Cyrus's cabin. A serious fight had obviously taken place there. None of us had much furniture—as we'd had to build it all by hand—but what little there had been was smashed to pieces.

Erica held a rag in her hand that reeked of chloroform, indicating that Cyrus had been overwhelmed and then knocked out.

An outboard motor suddenly roared to life close by, in the direction of the boat dock: The enemy, getting away.

Erica bolted toward the dock.

And before I could even think twice about the sanity of what I was doing, I ran after her.

NAUTICAL MANEUVERS

Spy School Satellite Facility

Kenai Fjords National Park, Alaska

July 17

1030 hours

The boat dock was located on a small peninsula that had been created during the last ice age by one of the nearby glaciers. Geologically, the landform was a moraine, a mass of rocks and sediment that the glacier had pushed in front of it. When the ice age ended and the earth began warming again, the glacier shrank, leaving a large, deep basin behind the moraine. Eventually, part of the moraine had collapsed, allowing seawater to fill the basin, but some of it still poked above the surface: a low, arcing ridge of loose rock that jutted into the fjord. It was like a miniature version of Cape Cod in Massachusetts, which had been created in the exact same way, but by a significantly larger glacier.

For the past few thousand years, the glaciers had retreated at a pace that was, well . . . glacial. But with climate change, the pace had picked up dramatically. The glacier nearest to our camp had shrunk by half a mile in less than a decade, while the considerably bigger one at the end of the fjord was constantly shedding sheets of ice.

Erica and I raced through the woods from our camp and scrambled to the top of the moraine. A small inflatable Zodiac boat was motoring across the calm waters of the fjord. There were four men in it, only three of whom were conscious. The fourth was sprawled out so haphazardly that one of his legs was dangling over the side. I couldn't see his face but presumed it was Cyrus.

Several oars jutted out over the other side, which explained why we hadn't heard the boat approaching. The enemy agents must have rowed it to the moraine. This would have been hard work but could have been done almost silently. Now, in the otherwise quiet fjord, the Zodiac's motor sounded as loud as a rocket launch.

Normally, there would have been several other watercraft at our small boat dock, mostly kayaks and canoes that we used for endurance training, but our enemies had scuttled and sunk them all so that we wouldn't be able to follow them.

However, the Hale family was always prepared for emergencies. We had our own motorboat at camp, but it was tucked behind the massive trunk of a dead tree farther down the moraine, and then hidden under a camouflage tarp for extra protection. Sure enough, our enemies had missed it. The motorboat was much bigger and faster than our enemies' Zodiac, powerful enough to get us to the closest town if needed (although it was much faster to take a helicopter, which was what Alexander and Catherine were using for their supply run). The boat was an aerodynamic sliver with a small pilothouse and a pair of three-hundred-horsepower engines.

Erica and I quickly yanked off the tarp, dragged the boat into the water, and hopped aboard. Within seconds, Erica had the engines fired up and we were in pursuit.

Behind us, Mike and Zoe emerged from the forest, heading for the moraine, panting heavily after their long run down the mountain. But we were already on our way.

Our motors roared even louder than those of the Zodiac, alerting our enemies that we were approaching.

The men turned toward us, and even from a distance, I could see their eyes go wide with surprise. Obviously, none of them had expected us to have an emergency backup boat, not to mention one that was so fast.

It was only now that I realized I didn't know what the next part of our plan was.

"Um . . . Erica?" I asked. "What are we supposed to do once we catch up to them?"

"We do to them what they did to Grandpa. Knock them senseless." Despite the challenge of this task, Erica spoke about it in the casual way that a normal person might have said they were going to drop by the post office.

I gulped. Even though I had been training hard lately, I was still wary about hand-to-hand combat. I had improved enough to beat most normal people in a fight, but enemy agents weren't normal people. "Er . . . there's three of them."

"I know. I can count."

"But there's only two of us. And I'm, well . . ."

"Pathetic at fighting?"

"I was going to say not that competent. But yes. Maybe we should go back for Mike and Zoe? Then we'd outnumber the bad guys."

"That'd take too much time. And besides, I can handle this."

"Are you sure? Those guys are very big. The guy at the stern looks like a Sasquatch without any hair."

"Fine with me. That'll just make them overconfident, and they'll underestimate us. Which will give me an advantage. Also, I have *this*." Erica popped open a storage compartment and took out an electric cattle prod. We had many of these at camp. Cyrus and Erica had souped them up so that they could render an attacking bear unconscious with one jab.

"Oh," I said. "Is there another one of those for me?"

"Yes, but I'm not going to give it to you."

"Why not?"

"Because there's a decent chance you'll zap yourself with it by mistake and turn yourself into a gibbering pile of jelly."

"Good point. Is there anything I can do to help?"

"Just stay out of my way and offer moral support."

"Okay." I still wasn't crazy about this plan, but I knew from experience that I wasn't going to change Erica's mind.

Besides, we were rapidly coming up on our enemies. They had now reached the center of the fjord, well away from its mountainous shores. The bad guys' original surprise at seeing us had faded, although they didn't seem to be preparing for a fight. At first, I figured this was because they were—as Erica had predicted—underestimating us. Which made sense. After all, we were merely two teenagers, and young teens at that, while the three of them had the musculature of people who had been consuming steroids since birth. But as we came closer, I noticed they were all smirking knowingly, like poker players with aces up their sleeve.

A second thought came to me that should have occurred to me earlier.

"Where did these guys come from?" I asked.

"I'm guessing Russia," Erica replied knowingly. "The lettering on their Zodiac is Cyrillic, and they dress like FSB." FSB was short for Federalnaya Sluzhba Bezopasnosti, which meant "Federal Security Service." The FSB was Russia's counterintelligence agency, their equivalent of the CIA. It had been created to replace the infamous KGB, which had operated throughout the Cold War, although plenty of old-time KGB operatives still worked for it.

"I didn't mean where did they come from *originally*," I said—although I was still interested in the answer. "I meant where did they come from *right now*? That boat isn't big enough to get them all the way here from the closest town, is it?"

Erica turned to me, looking worried. In her haste to rescue her grandfather, it appeared that she hadn't considered this either. "You're right. There must be—"

Before she could finish her statement, something began to rise out of the water ahead of us. Something very, very big.

At first, I thought it was a whale, because whales were relatively common in the fjord. Two days before, a humpback had breached so close to my kayak that I'd nearly been tossed by the waves it created. But the object was too blocky to be a whale, and it rose straight from the water, like an elevator, rather than propelling itself forward, as a whale would have done. It was dark and metallic, and water streamed off its sides.

Erica recognized what it was before I did, mostly because I couldn't believe what I was seeing. Then Erica did something I had rarely seen her do in the entire time I had known her: run away from a fight. She immediately spun the wheel of our boat, pulling a tight U-turn, and then sped back the way we had come.

I kept my eyes locked on the object that was rising from the fjord. "Is that a submarine?!"

"Yes," Erica replied, sounding unusually distressed. "Looks like a Yasen class, which definitely confirms these guys are Russian."

Behind us, the first part of the submarine I had seen—the conning tower—was now fully out of the water, and the body of the sub was emerging below it. The sub was big and bulbous, like a black lozenge that was a football field and a half in length. A hatch in the deck popped open, and two more Russians ascended through it. The three agents in the Zodiac pulled up alongside the sub and handed Cyrus's limp body over.

"They're putting your grandfather on that sub!" I told Erica.

"I know," she replied grimly.

"Then why are we running away from them? Cyrus needs our help!"

"We won't be much help to him if we're dead. We're armed with a cattle prod, and they have a nuclear submarine.

That's not a fair fight. If we survive the next ten minutes, then we'll rescue Cyrus."

"From a submarine? How are we going to do that?"

"It's not going to be easy."

Erica was speaking in her usual, levelheaded fashion, but I knew her well enough to see that she was legitimately concerned for her grandfather and upset that she'd had to turn tail. I even noticed her eyes watering, although it was possible that was a result of our speeding headlong into a cold wind.

The enormous ice field created its own weather. Living close to it was like standing next to an open freezer the size of Connecticut. Even now, on a sunny summer day, the wind that blew off the glaciers was frigid enough to make my teeth chatter.

Instead of heading back to the beach we had launched from, Erica was rounding the small peninsula and heading farther up the fjord, toward the largest glacier in the area. The Aialik Glacier was the one that had created the moraine our camp was situated on. It stretched across the end of the fjord two miles ahead of us, a wall of ice thirty times the size of the Hoover Dam.

I immediately realized what Erica's plan was. The expanse of moraine that had sunk below the waterline was hidden only a few feet beneath the surface, creating a barrier across the fjord so shallow that even whales couldn't pass over it. Which meant the submarine wouldn't be able to follow us into that area.

"You think you can get them to ground the sub on the moraine?" I asked.

"Possibly. If they're too intent on chasing us, maybe they won't realize there's a giant blockage right in front of them."

"And once they're grounded, we can gather the others for a counterattack."

"Exactly." Erica steered past the peninsula and over the sunken moraine. Even though the ridge of rock wasn't far below us, I couldn't see it. Water from glaciers was notoriously opaque, as the rivers of ice acted like gigantic bulldozers, scraping tons of dirt and rock into the ocean each day. Inland glaciers often had runoff streams so filled with silt that they were as gray as wet cement. In the fjord, the cloudy glacial water was diluted by seawater, but not enough to make it crystal clear. Since the rest of the fjord was quite deep, it made sense that the moraine, rising up suddenly in the midst of it, might catch the submariners by surprise, like an enormous underwater speed bump.

Although, even if that did work, defeating the Russians and getting Cyrus back would still be a daunting challenge. The sub was a floating fortress, and it certainly had a large crew of seamen operating it, whereas there were only four of us in camp at the moment. Our most talented fighter, after Erica, was currently unconscious and being held captive.

I spotted Mike and Zoe again as we raced past. They

were standing on the top of the moraine, gaping at the submarine in astonishment. Dwarfed by the landscape around them, they looked as small as ants—and even less menacing.

Behind us, the Russians had climbed into the sub with Cyrus and closed the hatch. They hadn't bothered to deflate the Zodiac and bring it aboard. Instead, they had abandoned it in their rush to pursue us. They didn't take the time to submerge, either. The sub simply came after us, its conning tower slicing through the water like the dorsal fin of a gigantic shark.

As Erica and I approached the glacier, we encountered the first icebergs. Hundreds of tons of ice calved off Aialik every day, often in great, dramatic cascades that rumbled like thunder as they plunged into the water. The thousands of resulting chunks of ice then floated freely through the fjord; the area around the glacier was loaded with them. An iceberg is usually about ten times larger beneath the surface than above, so even a berg that looked somewhat small was likely the size of a school bus. Any one of them could have given our little boat the *Titanic* treatment if we had run into it. So Erica had to concentrate on the path in front of us, while I kept a close eye on our enemy.

With its enormous nuclear-powered engines, the sub moved much faster than we did. It was swiftly approaching the moraine. I tensed with anticipation, hoping to see it run aground.

But that didn't happen. Just as it reached the sunken ridge, the submarine fired its reverse thrusters, the nautical equivalent of slamming the brakes. It didn't get stuck on the moraine, but it also couldn't follow us, which allowed me a sense of relief that we had escaped.

This lasted exactly two seconds.

Then the submarine fired a torpedo at us.

For an attack, it was surprisingly quiet. If I hadn't been watching the sub intently, I might not have even noticed it. There was merely a stream of bubbles that rose to the surface and moved very quickly in our direction.

"There's a torpedo coming for us!" I yelled, partly to be heard over the engines, and partly because I was horrified.

Erica glanced over her shoulder, then grew even more worried. "Nuts," she said. "I didn't think about that."

"You didn't?" I exclaimed, more accusingly than I had intended.

"No. Did *you*?"

"Er . . . no. But usually, you think of *everything*."

"Well, I didn't today. This is my first time facing a submarine."

"Do you know how to escape a torpedo attack?" I eyed the approaching stream of bubbles warily. It was coming toward us at a disturbingly high speed, as though we were being attacked by a giant Alka-Seltzer tablet.

"I have an idea," Erica replied, though not nearly as confidently as I'd hoped.

She suddenly veered sharply, taking us into an area that was chock-full of icebergs.

Behind us, the stream of bubbles also veered sharply.

"Looks like the torpedo is heat-seeking!" I reported.

"I figured," Erica muttered.

I didn't know why this particular section of the fjord had more icebergs than any other. It probably had something to do with wind or water currents. Whatever the case, there was a lot of ice in it, ranging widely in size. Some bergs were only a few feet across, while others were sheets as wide as a house. Seals and sea otters had hauled themselves out onto many of the larger ones, as they were the only safe haven from predators in the fjord; the water was rife with orcas, while the land was crawling with bears. In other circumstances, seeing all those adorable animals perched around us would have been heartwarming, but racing through the ice at top speed was harrowing—and having a torpedo in pursuit made it all a thousand times worse.

But Erica's plan was clever. Even though the torpedo was targeting the heat of our engines, following us through the icy maze was exceedingly challenging. Erica only had to slalom around a few bergs before the torpedo failed to negotiate one and slammed into it. The resulting explosion created a massive plume of water and instantly reduced the berg to a billion ice chips, which hailed down on us and the startled seals and otters.

Once again, my relief only lasted a few seconds. Then I spotted the other torpedoes.

"Two more on the way!" I announced, pointing at the twin streams of bubbles closing in on us.

"Of course," Erica grumbled, annoyed, then arced around an ice floe so large that a dozen seals were basking on it. Several of them were pups, only a few months old.

"Look out for the baby seals!" I yelled. "Don't let the torpedo blow them up!"

"I'm doing my best!" Erica yelled back. "You know how I feel about baby seals!"

I did. Despite her generally tough and cold exterior, Erica *loved* baby seals. And sea otters. And kittens. Back at our original spy school, her dormitory walls had been covered with posters of them (as well as one incredibly precious baby sloth)—a secret that I had been warned never to tell anyone under penalty of death. On many evenings in Alaska, after a hard day of training, I had found Erica on the moraine, gleefully watching baby seals through binoculars, although she told everyone else she was scouting for enemy agents.

So now, in addition to trying to speed through a labyrinth of icebergs at top speed and keep the torpedoes from catching up to us, Erica was also trying to steer clear of any bergs with lovable sea creatures on them, of which there were many. If her actions had led to the death of an innocent pinniped, she would have never forgiven herself. But to our dismay, it seemed as if every baby seal for miles was visiting the ice field, as though they were all on a preschool field trip to see the glacier.

I did my best to point them out as we zoomed through, screaming, "There's one! And another! And three more! And there's one with a baby otter! Oooh!"

"Don't say 'oooh,'" Erica warned. "This is stressful enough without you reminding me how cute they are!"

"Sorry."

Erica found a floe the size of a trailer home that was somehow devoid of adorable babies and hooked a tight curve around it. One of the torpedoes struck it and blew.

This blast was even larger than the first had been. So much ice flew through the air that it felt as though we were in a blizzard.

There was still one torpedo remaining.

Our path had taken us around a bend in the fjord. The mountain we had rappelled down earlier now stood between us and the submarine, blocking it from our sight—and hiding us from the sub as well. However, the torpedo was still doggedly tailing us. It somehow managed to avoid every bit of ice we set in its path and came closer and closer.

Which forced us much nearer to the glacier than we should have been.

There was no way to know when huge chunks of ice were going to calve. They did so regularly throughout the day. Every few minutes, a future berg would break off and tumble into the fjord, and the last place you wanted to be when that happened was directly beneath it. Or anywhere in the vicinity. A plummeting boulder of ice created waves that could easily swamp or tip our boat, and if we were tossed into the frigid water, it wouldn't be long before we froze to death. Or an orca ate us. Or both.

And yet, if we reversed course, the torpedo would slam into our boat and blow us to smithereens.

As we neared the glacier, the temperature plunged. Neither Erica nor I was dressed for the sudden shift. I began shivering again, and I noticed that the tips of Erica's fingers were turning blue.

A final ice floe bobbed in our path. Perched atop it were a mother seal and the most adorable seal pup in the universe, a baby animal that appeared to have been designed by a cuteness generator cranked to the highest level. Even Erica, who was struggling to maintain a cool demeanor, couldn't help but sigh, "Awwww."

Although every second counted, she still made a wide arc around the floe to prevent the torpedo from smashing into it. Which meant the torpedo gained precious ground. But I couldn't be upset with Erica; if anything had happened to the seal pup, I would have been emotionally devastated.

Unfortunately, now there was a very good chance that we were going to be *physically* devastated. The torpedo came screaming through the water at us.

Erica cut left at the last second, coming up directly against the giant wall of ice. The torpedo couldn't quite make the tight turn. In open water, it would have had room to correct, but now it clipped the glacier and exploded.

The resulting blast ripped out a chunk of ice the size of my house and pelted us with slush. The wave lifted us up from behind and nearly toppled us, but Erica expertly kept our boat upright. No more torpedoes were en route. It looked as though we were safe.

Then we heard the thunder.

The glacier, rattled by the blast at its base, started to calve in a major way. Cracks shot through it, making it look like a broken window as big as a skyscraper. Directly over our heads, massive sheets of ice quivered ominously.

"Drive!" I screamed.

"I'm trying!" Erica screamed back. She gunned the engines as hard as she could, although due to the heaving seas, our rear propellers had been lifted from the water.

Ten stories above us, the ice began to fall.

Our boat sank back into the water, and the propellers finally found purchase. We rocketed away from the glacier just as the first bits of ice plunked into the fjord.

From behind us came the loudest noise I had ever heard in my life.

In my adventures with spy school, I had ridden an airboat without earplugs, dangled from whirring helicopters, and even been in an abandoned coal mine when a rocket blasted off. All those things sounded like hushed whispers compared to the noise of a glacier coming apart at close range. The boom was so loud, my bones vibrated like tuning forks.

A sheet of ice as wide and flat as a Walmart parking lot sheared off the glacier and cannonballed into the water behind us, creating a tsunami. We raced ahead of it back through the ice field at high speed. All the adorable seal pups and otters abandoned ship, diving into the fjord as their ice floes were swept up by the wave.

A small island sat ahead of us, a jagged peak of shale poking out of the fjord. Erica aimed directly for it.

More gigantic chunks of ice were tearing free from the glacier and plunging into the fjord, making the wave swell even larger. It was now so big that the surface of the water around us was tilted like a ski slope. Hundreds of ice floes tobogganed down it. I caught sight of a startled harbor seal riding one, its eyes even bigger than usual.

Erica shot past the island, turned behind the far shore, and cut the engine.

The island acted like a wedge, cleaving the tsunami in half. The two large waves swept past us on both flanks of the island, leaving a relatively calm patch of water on the back side. Erica had cleverly positioned us in this safe harbor. We were still jostled about but were ultimately well protected.

Beyond the island, the fjord widened dramatically. The big waves dissipated and broke apart, sloshing against the rocky shores and leaving the ice floes bobbing up and down.

All around us, seal pups and otters poked their heads from the water, unharmed but seeming very confused.

Our race for safety had taken us back to where we could see the moraine again.

The submarine was no longer in sight. The Russians hadn't even stuck around to see if they'd blown us from the water, most likely presuming we couldn't escape.

If anyone else besides Erica had been driving, we probably wouldn't have.

But the situation was still bad. The Russians were gone. And they had Cyrus Hale.

TRANSMISSION

Spy School Satellite Facility

Kenai Fjords National Park, Alaska

July 17

1115 hours

"Why would the Russians want to kidnap your grandfather?" Zoe asked.

"There's hundreds of reasons," Erica replied sadly. "I just don't know which one is right."

She was hurrying toward Cyrus's cabin from the rocky beach, where we had docked the speedboat. Mike and Zoe had been waiting for us there, astonished by everything they had witnessed.

Erica and I were drenched from being pelted by water,

hail, and slush, while Mike and Zoe had been hit by the remnants of the tsunami. A four-foot wave had swamped the beach, soaking them to their waists—as well as submerging three black bears that had been rooting for clams. The bears had survived, although they had been very startled and bolted for high ground.

Our shoes were squelching, and I was feeling a nasty chill from my damp clothes. But Erica insisted we had no time to change into dry ones. With every second, the Russians were spiriting Cyrus farther away.

"Grandpa crossed paths with the Russians many times during his days in the CIA," Erica explained. "There's a lot of bad blood between them." She stormed into Cyrus's cabin.

With the door broken, the local wildlife had already invaded. A trio of marmots was devouring Cyrus's stash of granola while a mink was making off with his beef jerky. They scattered as we entered.

Each of our cabins was the same, a simple wooden square with basic, handmade furnishings and a wood-burning stove for heat. As I had noted earlier, the room was a mess after Cyrus's fight against the Russians, but now I had a much better look at it. His bed had collapsed, his dresser was flattened, and his single chair appeared to have been smashed over someone's head. His belongings were strewn everywhere.

Erica immediately assigned each of us a quadrant and ordered us to start searching. We went to work, sifting through the wreckage.

"What are we looking for?" Mike asked.

"I'm hoping Grandpa left a clue as to where he thought the Russians might take him," Erica replied, sifting through the busted remains of the dresser. "Or *why* they were coming for him at all."

"Any idea what this clue might look like?" I warily examined a pile of Cyrus's long underwear.

"Unfortunately, no." Erica uncovered a pair of her grandfather's cargo shorts and rooted through the pockets. "It could be almost anything."

"I've got a note!" Zoe exclaimed suddenly. She triumphantly held up a handwritten piece of paper she had found under the ruins of the bed.

The rest of us turned to her expectantly. "Is it a message for us?" Erica asked.

Zoe took a closer look at it and frowned. "No. It's just a love letter to your grandmother."

Erica grew intrigued. "A love letter? From my grandfather? That doesn't sound like him at all. It must be some sort of code. What's it say?"

Zoe began to read it. "'My dearest Mary, I miss you terribly. I long for your glorious smile, the delightful sound of your laughter, the smell of your hair, the feel of your lips against mine . . .'"

"That definitely sounds like a love note to me," I said.

Erica shook her head. "Grandpa doesn't have a romantic bone in his body. There's no way he would ever write something that sappy."

"Sappy?" Mike echoed. "That's good stuff." He snatched the note from Zoe's hands and looked it over. "I ought to steal some of this next time I write to Trixie."

Erica gave him a look of disgust. "If you ever write anything like that to my sister, I'll kill you."

Mike gulped, unsure if the threat was exaggerated or not. He had met Erica's younger sister a few weeks earlier, and the two of them had instantly fallen for each other—which most of the Hale family was unhappy about. This was partly because, until that point, the Hales had kept Trixie in the dark about what the family business really was, but Mike and I had accidentally spilled the beans. And partly because the Hales didn't like the idea of Trixie dating anyone, let alone an agent-in-training. Trixie had wanted to come to Alaska with us, but the Hales had felt it was too dangerous and sent her to a boarding school in Utah under an assumed name. She and Mike were writing letters every day, but Cyrus was censoring them; each one Mike got from Trixie was so full of redactions that it was barely legible.

Erica took her grandfather's note from Mike and read more of it. "'The glow of your eyes warms me like the summer sun on a day in Paris in June. The sound of your voice puts Beethoven's symphonies to shame.' Blech. This has to be a secret message of some sort. Maybe the *real* message is in invisible ink." She squinted at the paper.

"Maybe your grandfather has a side to him you don't know about," I said. "A lot of the Hale family has secrets like that." I gave her a sharp look, so she would realize I was talking about *her* and her fondness for posters with adorable baby animals. And gingham tea cozies.

Erica got my point, although she seemed unsettled by this new, romantic side of her grandfather. "I suppose you might be right." She pocketed the love letter, then said, "And if that's the case, then we're back to square one. So keep looking for a *real* message."

We all returned to searching our quadrants. I was inspecting the wall for hidden panels when I noticed Zoe was sniffling close by.

"Are you upset about something?" I asked her.

"No," she said quickly. "I'm just having an allergic reaction."

"You're not allergic to anything except blue cheese," Erica informed her. Erica never forgot anything about anyone.

"I think I might be developing new allergies," Zoe claimed, although I got the sense that she wasn't telling the truth. "There's a lot of pollen in the air today. Or maybe I'm getting a chill from wearing these wet clothes."

"Me too," Mike said, then looked at Erica. "Are you *sure* we don't have time to change? I chafe when I wear wet undies."

"The Russians have captured my grandfather!" Erica snapped. "Every second counts! If *your* grandfather was captured by the Russians, would you want me wasting time putting on dry underwear?"

"Honestly, yes," Mike replied. "I wouldn't want your abilities to fight for my grandfather's freedom to be compromised by chafing." He paused to adjust his undergarments, then added, "Or by having your wet undies ride up your buttocks. It's *very* uncomfortable."

"You know who's really uncomfortable right now?" Erica said coldly. "My grandfather. He's trapped in a submarine with a whole lot of Russians who probably have advanced degrees in torture. I already failed him once today. I'm not going to do it again. I'm going to figure out where he's headed, and I'm going to get him back, with or without you."

I paused my search for hidden panels and turned to Erica. "You didn't fail your grandfather."

"Yes I did. I allowed him to get captured."

"Cyrus allowed himself to get captured," I corrected. "You did everything in your power to save him."

"It wasn't enough." Erica grumpily kicked aside some crumpled bedsheets. "I should have been better prepared for trouble."

"This isn't your fault," I insisted.

"That's right," Zoe added supportively.

Erica glowered, obviously not convinced.

Despite his discomfort, Mike returned to searching the room, rather than going to change.

So did I. I resumed my hunt for secret panels, rapping my knuckles on the wall. I knew it was probably futile, but there weren't any other places left in my small quadrant to search.

The section of the wall I knocked on made a hollow thunk, as though there was an empty space behind it. "Hey!" I said excitedly. "I think there's a secret compartment here."

Erica immediately hurried to my side.

"Listen." I rapped on the wall where I thought the secret compartment might be, then the wall a foot away. The sounds were distinctly different.

"I think you've got something." Erica considered the potential secret spot for a few seconds, then pushed on a knothole in the wood.

A hidden panel in the wall popped open.

It was only four inches across, but that was more than enough room to conceal what Cyrus had hidden there: his mobile phone.

We all gasped with excitement. Erica's foul mood instantly vanished. "Nice work!" she told me, then grabbed the phone. It was locked, but of course, Erica knew her grandfather's pass code; either he had shared it with her, or, being Erica, she had figured it out at some point. It opened directly to the photos, where Cyrus had recently recorded a video.

"He left us a message!" Zoe announced exuberantly.

I felt equally enthusiastic.

But then Erica played the video.

Cyrus Hale was an incredible spy, but he was inept with modern technology. In previous missions, he had always struggled to work anything on his phone: texts, his alarm, the calculator. But the thing he had the most trouble with, by far, was the camera. Any time he tried to take a photo or film a video, it was blurry, or his finger was blocking the lens, or he had the camera aimed at his disturbingly hairy nostrils instead of his intended subject. Now, in his haste to record a message for us, certainly aware that an enemy was coming for him, he had botched the job worse than usual.

For starters, he once again had the camera aimed the wrong way. So instead of recording his face, he had filmed a random spot on the floor.

"I don't have time to explain what's going on," he began. "But if things go wrong, you'll probably find me at—"

That was all we got, as Cyrus's next words suddenly grew distorted, as though each syllable was being stretched out.

"Oh no!" Erica cried. "He recorded himself in slow motion!"

In the video, Cyrus appeared to recognize that he had done something wrong, because the camera got fumbled about as he tried to figure out how to correct the situation.

"This isn't a problem," Mike said. "It's no big deal to switch the video back to normal mode." With that, he tapped the screen a few times, resetting the video speed.

Only now Cyrus was so aggravated that he was screaming obscenities at the phone. Or rather, he was screaming one particular word over and over in frustration. A word that my parents weren't fans of me using, but which they also said repeatedly when something electronic wasn't working. (In my father's case, it was usually the TV remote.)

Then, on the video, Cyrus suddenly fell silent. He had actually managed to aim the camera toward his face for once, so we saw him glance toward the door of his cabin with concern. After that, the image whipped wildly, which was probably the motion of Cyrus taking the phone to his secret hiding place, and then the video stopped abruptly.

I could presume that, in the following seconds, Cyrus had closed the secret panel, the Russians had barged into his cabin, a fight had ensued, and Cyrus had been knocked unconscious.

Erica sighed. "My grandfather *really* needs to learn how to use his phone."

I felt the same sense of exasperation. Instead of giving us the information we needed, Cyrus had squandered his precious time trying to figure out how to operate his camera. If he had just used a pencil and paper, we would have known where he'd been taken.

But then something occurred to me. "Can you rewind that video? I want to hear what Cyrus said again."

"I think we've heard enough," Erica said sullenly.

"Maybe not," I told her.

Erica begrudgingly rewound the video fifteen seconds and played it again.

Once again, Cyrus's curses filled the air. "Listen closely," I said.

It wasn't that easy to discern Cyrus's words, partly because he was waving the camera around wildly, and partly because they had originally been recorded in slow motion, so they were still somewhat garbled. But as we focused, something new became evident.

"I don't think he's cursing at all," Zoe said. "He's saying something else."

"Flocking?" I suggested, trying to make sense of it.

"Farting?" Mike proposed.

"Fort King!" Erica exclaimed. "He's saying 'Fort King'!"

She suddenly turned away from us and darted back across the room.

"What's Fort King?" Zoe asked.

Erica dug through a pile of Cyrus's belongings that had been knocked to the floor, searching for something. "The Russians have had outposts in Alaska since the 1700s. Much longer than the Americans. And Grandpa always claimed that they'd held on to some of them long after America bought Alaska in 1867. I'm betting that Fort King is one of those outposts. . . . Aha!" She knocked aside a tube of denture cream to uncover a weather-beaten map, which she held up triumphantly. "Grandpa kept track of all the Russian sites on here!"

She unfolded the map carefully, as it was so old and creased that it looked as though it might crumble into dust at any moment. It appeared that Cyrus had been using it for decades and, given his distaste for new technology, I was betting he had no digital backup.

Erica gently set the map on the canted mattress of Cyrus's busted bed, and we gathered around to inspect it.

It was an army-issue map, which Cyrus had amended in red ink, marking a dozen locations of Russian bases.

"All of them are on the coast," Zoe observed.

"Makes sense," Erica said. "The Russians never pushed that far into the interior of Alaska, even when they owned it. It's difficult to explore, and the weather's crummy most of the year. Even the Americans didn't get most of our roads built until the 1970s."

"Plus, there's a couple thousand miles of coastline," I noted, looking over the map. "And a lot of it is awfully remote. It probably wasn't too hard for the Russians to find places where a fort would be overlooked. At least until surveillance satellites came along." The southern coast of the state, where we were, was an extremely corrugated line filled with thousands of fjords, bays, inlets, and coves, while to the west, the Alaska Peninsula and the archipelago of the Aleutian Islands extended over a thousand miles from the mainland into the Bering Sea. Most of the land was nearly uninhabited. Cyrus had told me there were far more bears living out there than humans.

"There!" Zoe pointed to a mark Cyrus had made on the map, along with the words "Fort King" and "Czar krepost," which was most likely the Russian name for it. It was located on the northwest shore of Kodiak, an island with a coast so crumpled, it looked kind of like a pine cone that someone had stepped on.

"That's only about a hundred miles away from us!" Mike said. "In Alaska terms, that's like being around the corner."

"But there's still no way to get to it." I indicated the blue expanse of the Gulf of Alaska that stretched between our location and Fort King. "Our boat isn't big enough to take us that far, and even if it was, it's still nowhere near as fast as that Russian submarine."

"That's all true," Erica said thoughtfully, "except for one thing: We *do* have one way to get there."

I realized what she was talking about, and my blood ran cold.

"No," I said. "That's way too dangerous."

"We have to," Erica replied. "My grandfather is in danger—and it's the only way to save him."

AVIATION

Somewhere over the Gulf of Alaska

July 17

1300 hours

The helicopter that Erica had been learning to fly
was a forty-year-old battle-scarred trainer. Her father had
been teaching her; Alexander wasn't a great spy, but he had
turned out to be a competent helicopter pilot. However, he
had insisted that the trainer was only capable of short flights
and was never to be flown more than a mile from our camp;
there was a significant chance that it might fall apart in mid-
flight and put whoever was on board in need of a rescue
operation.

"Can't we wait for your parents to get back from their

supply run?" I asked as we looted our storage sheds for assault gear. "They have the *good* helicopter. The one that can actually make it to Kodiak."

"There's no time," Erica insisted.

"We should at least call them," Zoe said.

"I will," Erica replied. "But they're at least an hour away, and every second the Russians have Grandpa, his life is in danger. I don't know what they're going to do with him once they get him to Fort King, but I can promise you they won't be throwing him a tea party."

It was hard to make any argument against that. Over the past few months, Erica had risked her life to save my parents several times, so it seemed only fair that I help rescue her grandfather. (My enemies had tried to use my parents as leverage to prevent me from thwarting evil schemes; now, for their safety, they were in the Witness Protection Program in a nice suburb of San Diego and seemed to be doing well. Dad was running the local farmer's market, while Mom volunteered at the safari park, and both had taken up golf and yoga.)

Despite Erica's insistence that every second counted, even she realized we had to take the time to properly equip ourselves. We needed to be prepared to infiltrate a Russian fortress—and any venture into the Alaskan wilderness required significant gear. The weather could change dramatically within short distances—or even in the same place within brief periods of time, so we grabbed rain jackets, waterproof pants, fleeces, gloves, thermal underwear, and sunblock. Then we needed weapons, explosives, snacks (it was never a good idea to face the enemy when you were hypoglycemic)—and the three basics of Alaskan travel: muck boots, mosquito repellent, and bear spray.

The muck boots were necessary because a great deal of Alaska was soggy. The terrain was filled with lakes, ponds, rivers, creeks, streams, bogs, swamps, and mud. And it rained a lot, so even dry land could turn squishy within minutes. No matter how much you tried to waterproof hiking boots, they usually ended up sodden. Muck boots were clunky and ungainly, but at least they kept your toes dry.

I was no stranger to mosquitoes, but they were far worse in Alaska than any other place I'd been. Thankfully, they weren't too bad around our camp, which sat in the path of a glacial breeze that whisked mosquitoes away, but in other locations, they would make coordinated attacks in great, humming clouds. Within seconds, you'd be covered in ravenous bloodsuckers. I'd read that in some parts of Alaska, animals like caribou could lose up to a pint of blood a day to them. Cyrus had requisitioned extra-strength repellent from the military, which fended off most of the little jerks.

Bear spray was very similar to the pepper spray that

city people used to repel muggers, except it was more concentrated—as bears are considerably bigger than humans—and designed to be spread over a much larger area. It came in pressurized aerosol cans about the same size as shaving cream canisters, which had caused Alexander Hale considerable agony one morning when he got them mixed up. Luckily, most bears weren't very aggressive. Even with the large population around our camp, none of us had ever needed to resort to using bear spray, but we still carried it with us at all times. You never knew when you might run into a rogue grizzly—or even more dangerous, a protective mama bear with cubs.

We crammed everything we could into backpacks, and then, to Mike's relief, Erica relented and let us change out of our damp clothes. She said it was so that we could properly outfit ourselves for action, but I think that her wet underwear was chafing a bit too. Mike, Zoe, and I dressed in camouflage, while Erica wore her standard action outfit: a sleek black sheath accented with a chic utility belt. (Erica didn't need camouflage to hide herself; she was so stealthy, she could have vanished into the shadows wearing neon leggings and an aloha shirt.) She wore muck boots as well, but somehow, she could even make those seem stylish.

I brought my own utility belt, which had been a gift from Erica's mother, although mine wasn't nearly as well stocked as Erica's. She had things like razor wire, explosives, and cyanide capsules, while, for my own safety, I carried less dangerous things, like a compass and dental floss. (Oral hygiene is always important.)

Thanks to our training, we did all of this in under ten minutes, and so, not long after discovering Cyrus's video, we found ourselves on a harrowing helicopter ride across the Gulf of Alaska. I had never been up in the trainer before, because it had always looked to me like it might break apart in a strong wind. It was usually parked in a bog on the banks of a glacial pond near camp, and it was held together with baling wire and duct tape. The interior was even worse. There was no rear seat; Zoe and I had to perch atop our gear in a space so cramped that our noses almost touched. (Mike got the front seat because he was taller than either of us.) Despite this, we could still barely hear each other, due to the whirr of the rotors and the rattling of the old machinery. Erica and Mike both had noise-cancelling headsets with built-in microphones so that they could communicate, but the trainer was only equipped with two of them. For Zoe and me, it sounded like we were in an oil drum full of spare parts as it rolled down a hill.

The helicopter also shook a lot, as though every piece of it was in the process of coming off. And Erica's flying style wasn't helping things. Erica was normally adept at handling any type of moving vehicle, but she was still new to flying a helicopter, and it showed. Perhaps, if she had been in a *real* helicopter, rather than a rickety bucket of bolts like the trainer, the ride might have been smoother, but instead, it was nausea inducing. Things had been dicey right from the start; Erica had flown too close to the forest and buzz-cut the tops off a few pine trees with the rotors. Then we had nearly slammed into a small mountain. But we had eventually made it back down the fjord to the sea.

The good news about being over open water was that there weren't any obstacles to crash into. The bad news was that if anything went wrong, our chances of survival were virtually nonexistent. The trainer was too small to hold a heavy emergency raft, and we were way too far from shore to swim to safety.

And if we actually managed to survive our perilous journey across the ocean, then we would still have to confront the Russian agents who had tried to kill me and Erica with a torpedo attack a few hours earlier.

It was all very disturbing to think about. And yet, it was hard to focus on anything else, given that the helicopter was juddering so hard I thought that my brains were going to vibrate out through my ears. The trainer wasn't very fast, and the weather was crummy. Even though it was still summer, arctic winds whistled through the numerous cracks in the hull and buffeted the fragile craft so hard that it didn't move in a beeline so much as the jouncing, herky-jerky pattern of a housefly. It was a long, jarring trip, during which multiple screws and bolts shook loose from the fuselage and clattered to the floor of the cabin, making me fear that, at any second, the bottom might drop out of the copter. Eventually, I decided that I had to do something to distract myself. So even though I was sure Zoe wouldn't want to have the conversation, I asked, "What was so upsetting to you about Cyrus's love letter?"

She did a decent job of pretending that she had no idea what I was talking about. "What do you mean? I wasn't upset."

"Yes you were. You weren't sniffling because of allergies. Erica was right: The only allergy you have is to blue cheese—and it doesn't give you the sniffles. It makes your ears swell up like balloons."

Zoe winced, aware she'd been caught. Then she glanced toward Erica and Mike, uneasy about continuing the conversation within earshot of them.

"Don't worry," I assured her. "They can't hear us. The helicopter's too loud. And they have headphones."

"Doesn't matter. Erica could hear a mouse burp from three miles away."

"Not from this chopper, she couldn't." To demonstrate, I raised my voice and said, "Erica! You stink!"

Erica showed no response. Not only could she not hear

me, but she was also laser focused on keeping the helicopter from crashing into the sea.

I returned my attention to Zoe. "So? Why was the letter upsetting?"

Zoe wavered a few more moments before answering. Then she dropped her guard and said, "I was just thinking that no one was ever going to write *me* a love letter like that."

"Of course someone will."

"You don't know that for sure. Maybe I won't ever meet anyone who feels like that about me."

"That's not true. Zoe, you're amazing."

"And yet, not amazing enough for *you*."

I grimaced in response to this, feeling terrible. A few months before, I had discovered that Zoe liked me. At the time, Erica had told me that she thought being in a relationship with anyone was a bad idea, and so I had toyed with the idea of dating Zoe. But then Erica had changed her mind, and I had immediately jumped at the chance to date her, leaving Zoe in the lurch.

"You don't know what it's like, being at spy school alone now," Zoe went on. "I mean, back at regular spy school, there were plenty of people who weren't dating. It wasn't a big deal to be single. But now that we've relocated to Alaska, you're with Erica, Alexander and Catherine are back together, Mike's with Trixie . . ."

"But they can't see each other. . . ."

"Doesn't matter. They're still a couple. They send each other goopy romantic love notes every chance they get. Even *Cyrus* has someone, and he's the most crotchety man on earth and has ten pounds of hair growing in his ears. But I'm all alone."

"That's not because you aren't a great person. I mean, Murray Hill has a *huge* crush on you. . . ."

"Yuck. Murray's the worst."

"But he's still a person. And Warren Reeves fell for you too."

"Double yuck. Warren was a traitor."

"I'm just saying that you've had suitors. They were *terrible* suitors, but still. . . . This isn't about any failure on your part. It's just the circumstances."

"Tell me about it. How am I ever going to meet anyone, living out in the boonies? The only new people I've even seen in the past month just tried to kill you."

I put my hand on hers in what I hoped was a comforting way and said, "This isn't going to be permanent."

"But it could be a *really* long time. Months, at least. Maybe even years. Our training is supposed to last until we're in our late teens. Who am I supposed to date during that time? A seal? A bear? Maybe I'll meet a nice orca some-day. . . ."

I had no idea what to say. I had never thought about what it must have been like for Zoe to be there with the rest of us, and now I felt terrible about that. All I could offer were useless clichés that sounded straight out of a greeting card. "I can imagine things look pretty bleak now, but this isn't the way things will always be. Someday you'll meet someone. Someone great."

"I don't want to meet someone someday. I want to meet someone *now*. I'm *lonely*, Ben. And it's going to be a million times worse once winter comes and it's dark twenty hours a day. That's not exactly a cure for depression."

"Land ho!" Mike yelled suddenly, as loud as he possibly could, to make sure that we heard him over all the noise.

Sure enough, in the distance, Kodiak Island rose from the sea. It might have been partly due to my relief that we were close to land again, but I instantly thought it was one of the most beautiful places I had ever seen. There were rugged snow-capped peaks, lush green forests, and glistening blue bays.

But most importantly, it was solid ground. It didn't appear that the trainer was going to last much longer. As we neared the island, the engine began to cough and wheeze, and the entire craft shuddered. If Kodiak had been another mile from the mainland, we might not have made it.

A small town lined the waterfront on the closest side of

the island to us. As we approached, I noted a few places where we could safely set down—but to my dismay, Erica passed right over them and continued onward across the island.

Mike was obviously just as concerned, because he shouted, "Why didn't you land?"

"That town's on the wrong side of the island from Fort King!" Erica shouted back. "There's no way across!" She pointed to the ground below.

Sure enough, there didn't appear to be a single road that crossed the island. In fact, there were almost no roads at all. It was just a pristine expanse of mountains, forests, and ponds, which was lovely from an environmental point of view, but disconcerting where safety was concerned.

"There's no place to land!" Mike shouted, echoing my thoughts.

"I'm sure we'll find somewhere closer to Fort King!" Erica replied.

"I don't think the trainer's going to make it much further!" Zoe hollered.

"This chopper's in better shape than you think!" Erica insisted, then patted the dashboard reassuringly.

That section of the dashboard promptly broke off.

"Whoops," Erica said.

The trainer's wheezing and shuddering grew worse.

I pressed myself against the window, desperately searching

for a safe landing spot, but all I could see below us was a thick, impenetrable forest.

Kodiak Island wasn't very wide. We could already see the far side, crinkled with fjords. Deep ravines ran from the glaciers that had carved them down to the sea.

"There!" Mike shouted, pointing to a break in the trees ahead. "That looks like a decent place to land!"

"Got it!" Erica replied, and veered that way.

The engine suddenly made a loud bang and then started smoking. Several bolts tore free from the fuselage with such force that they ricocheted about the cabin. The metal shell of the trainer tore like paper, letting a cold blast of air inside.

The spot Mike had noticed ahead wasn't a nice, grassy clearing. It was a bog, which was going to be much trickier to land on. As we approached, I could see the ground was thick with underbrush.

"Hang on!" Erica warned. "This might be rough!"

She brought us in low, trailing smoke and bits of hardware. We were ten feet above the ground when the chopper made a death rattle. The engine conked out and burst into flames, and we dropped into the bog with a splat.

The tail of the chopper immediately snapped off and plunked into the mud behind us, leaving a large new opening in the fuselage. Zoe and I sprang out through it, while

Erica and Mike leapt through the doors. There wasn't enough time to unload all our equipment. We grabbed what was close at hand and then fled the burning chopper. The underbrush snagged at our legs, and the spongy earth sucked at our boots, making it difficult to run, but we did so anyhow, hurrying to put space between us and the trainer.

We were about thirty yards away from it when it blew up. The explosives we had brought along ignited and ripped the craft apart.

We all dove for safety into the underbrush. The fuselage instantly turned to shrapnel and whistled over our heads. The main rotor blades tore off and cartwheeled through the air before embedding in a spruce tree at the edge of the bog like an enormous throwing star.

We got back to our feet, dripping with bog water, and considered the smoking hull of our helicopter.

"I think we should take a boat back to the mainland," Mike suggested.

Zoe and I immediately seconded this.

"First things first," Erica told us. "Let's find Grandpa." She headed across the bog in the direction of Fort King.

We followed her. The ground was soupy and stank of decaying plant life. It felt—and smelled—like we were walking across the world's biggest cow patty. With each step, the viscous terrain made silly slorping noises.

Even though I wasn't pleased by how our flight had ended, Erica's risky decision had paid off. We were now relatively close to Fort King. Once we made it out of the bog, it was only a short hike through the forest until we came to the edge of a cliff that overlooked the inlet we had been targeting. The inlet formed the lower end of one of the steep glacial ravines I had seen from the air. Our high vantage point gave us an excellent view of the entire area.

However, Fort King wasn't there.

"I don't see anything," I muttered sadly, fearing that we had just made that traumatic helicopter ride for no reason.

"Look closer," Erica told me, then pointed to a rocky beach at the end of the inlet.

I looked closer. The inlet was beautiful, a finger of crystal-blue water flanked by rocky cliffs, although at the far end from the sea, the slope was gentler and coated with dense forest. A wide stream snaked down through the trees, cascading over mossy rocks until it reached the shoreline. It was a lovely, protected harbor.

I still did not see a fort.

Although I did see bears. *Lots* of bears. And they were startlingly big. So big that I thought my eyes were playing tricks on me. They appeared to be three times larger than the black bears that lived around our camp.

"Are those bears *normal?*" Mike asked, concerned.

"Because they look as if the Russians have jacked them up on steroids. Like, to make superbears."

"Why would the Russians make superbears?" Zoe asked.

"For protection," Mike replied. "To eat anyone who comes near their fort."

"They're Kodiak bears," Erica told us. "They're a sub-species of brown bear that only lives on this island—and they're unusually large because there's a lot for them to eat here."

I now noticed that the bears were all gathered around the stream, fishing for salmon. Salmon were born in lakes, swam downstream to the ocean to live most of their lives, and then after several years, they returned en masse to the exact same lakes where they had been born to spawn and die. No one understood how they did it. For most salmon, it wasn't an easy journey home; they had to fight their way uphill through the streams, leaping from one pool to the next—and every bear in Alaska knew they were coming. The salmon were easy pickings. The bears were casually swatting them out of the stream. As I watched, one fish actually leapt from the water directly into the mouth of a waiting bear.

"I still don't see a fort," I said.

"It's right there," Erica told me, slightly exasperated, and then pointed to a copse of trees at the end of the inlet.

I looked even harder at it. Finally, I saw what Erica meant.

Tucked back deep in the woods was a simple log cabin. It must have been there for a very long time, because the forest had nearly swallowed it. The walls were covered in tangles of vines, while grass, moss, and even a few trees had taken root on the roof. There were no windows, and it was built into the slope of the hill behind it. Except for the sturdy wooden door, it was nearly invisible.

"That's not much of a fort," Mike stated.

"If it was much bigger, it'd be easy to see," Erica claimed. "But this blends in awfully well. Our government doesn't even seem to know that the Russians have kept using it all this time."

"Are you sure they've been using it?" I asked skeptically. "It looks abandoned."

"It's not," Erica informed me. "In fact, the Russians have Grandpa there right now."

I desperately wanted to ask how Erica knew this but hesitated, worried that asking the question would make it evident that I lacked her skills of observation.

Luckily, Zoe asked the question for me. "How do you know that?"

Erica sighed, clearly disappointed in Zoe, and then said, "It's obvious. There are wet drag marks and several sets of footprints on the ground leading from the inlet to the door, indicating that several people pulled an inflatable raft ashore recently. They must have come here in it from the sub, which is too big to fit in this inlet and is probably parked out in the ocean where we can't see it, while the raft has been deflated and hidden in the woods. And as for how I know the fort's been in use, there are at least a dozen security cameras in the woods around it. They're all relatively new, so they have been installed recently. And if there are cameras, there are probably also sensors as well, which is a big problem. Because if we're going to rescue Grandpa from there, we need the element of surprise."

"Not a problem," Mike said confidently. "I can get rid of the cameras."

Erica looked to him curiously. "What's your plan?"

"It's simple," Mike replied. "All I need is a slingshot and five cans of chocolate frosting."

INFILTRATION

Fort King

Kodiak Island

July 17

1330 hours

Mike was very smart and an excellent athlete, but the main reason the CIA had recruited him was his tendency to think outside the box. When faced with a problem, Mike often came up with a solution that wouldn't have occurred to anyone else.

For example, most people would have been daunted by the idea of approaching a secret fortress surrounded by high-tech security cameras and enormous bears. But to Mike, the bears were actually an asset.

"The only thing these bears are trying to do is consume calories so they can make it through the winter," he explained. (All of us had learned a great deal about bear behavior while being surrounded by so many of them over the last few weeks.) "So if we smear something full of calories, like chocolate frosting, on the cameras, the bears will take them out for us."

"That's a great plan," Zoe said. "Except for one thing: The closest supermarket is a hundred miles away. Where are we supposed to get chocolate frosting?"

"Right here." Mike opened the small backpack he'd managed to salvage from the helicopter and removed five cans of it.

"Why do you have so much frosting?" I asked.

"Because we need calories ourselves. We've been burning them like crazy on all those training hikes. And frosting is nature's perfect hiking food: fat, sugar, and chocolate. I asked Catherine to get me a few cans on the last supply run."

"And you didn't ever share any of it with us?" Zoe asked.

"Did you share any of the gummy worms you had Catherine secretly bring you last week?" Mike asked pointedly.

Zoe turned red. "You knew about that?"

"Yes. Just like I knew about Ben's secret stash of Twizzlers, and Erica's cache of raisins . . . which, by the way, are the lamest guilty pleasure of all time."

"Raisins are very sugary," Erica said defensively. "But also high in fiber and an excellent source of potassium."

"They're old grapes," Mike countered. "And they're nowhere near as delicious as chocolate frosting. I'm sure the bears would agree. I grabbed my last few cans back at our camp just in case we ended up stranded in the wilderness—but I'm willing to spare them to save Cyrus. Now all we have to do is get the frosting onto the cameras, which requires someone with excellent aim—and *this*." He removed a sling-shot from his pack, then tossed to it Erica.

The slingshot had come from our camp armory. It wasn't one of the crummy ones that were sold in toy stores. Instead, it had been specially designed for tactical combat use by a military contractor. The fork was made from high-grade aluminum rein-forced with tungsten strands, while the launching apparatus was an advanced elastic polymer. We had been training with them lately because slingshots were much quieter and lighter than guns and rarely broke down, as they had so few moving parts.

Not surprisingly, Erica was the best shot. Erica was profi-cient with any weapon, from peashooters to bazookas.

"Hold on," Zoe said. "Not to question the plan or any-thing, but . . . why go through the trouble to involve the bears at all? Why not just let Erica knock the cameras out with the slingshot and some stones?"

"Because if Erica simply knocks out the cameras, the

Russians will get suspicious," Mike explained. "And then they'll conclude there's an attack coming. But that won't be the case if they think the bears are causing the damage. Plus, if there are other sensors—like lasers or trip wires—it'll be best to have the bears trigger them, rather than us."

"Oh," Zoe said. "Good thinking."

"Thanks." Mike beamed proudly.

Erica grabbed the first can of frosting from him. "Let's get to work."

She led the way to the forested slope that descended to the inlet. We were just starting down when I noticed that I'd left something very important behind in my hurry to evacuate the helicopter.

"Does anyone have a spare can of bear spray?" I asked.

My friends all paused to check, then frowned.

"Er . . . no," Mike said. "I think I might have dropped mine in the bog."

"I forgot to pack any," Zoe admitted.

"I left mine back in the helicopter," Erica said. "Although I do have some cyanide in my utility belt."

"That's helpful," I noted sarcastically. "If the bears attack, I'll just propose a toast and then slip some poison into their drinks while they're not looking."

"We'll be all right," Erica insisted, and then continued down the slope toward the fort.

The rest of us dutifully followed her. As we descended, we tried to make enough noise so that we wouldn't startle any grizzlies that might be lurking in the woods—and yet, not so much noise that it would alert the Russians. It was intensely unsettling to be walking *toward* a large gathering of enormous bears, rather than doing the sensible thing and walking away from them. Especially when carrying five tins of chocolate frosting, which was like shouting "free candy" to a room full of kindergarteners.

Still, the bears were so distracted by the salmon run that they didn't seem to notice us—or perhaps they simply didn't care. But then, once we were positioned atop a rocky outcrop fifty yards from Fort King, Erica cracked open the first tin of frosting.

Bears have the best sense of smell of any land animal. Its seven times better than a bloodhound's. And their hearing is exceptionally keen as well. The moment that Erica ripped the foil cover off the tin and allowed the smell of chocolate to waft into the air, every bear in the area stopped what it was doing. They pricked up their ears, raised their noses, flared their nostrils, and—sensing the presence of sugar—huffed hungrily.

Mike, Zoe, and I leapt into action before the bears started coming our way. We each took a small stone, dipped it in frosting, rolled that into a round pellet, and handed it to Erica. Erica took the pellets as fast as we could make them, then used the slingshot to fire them at the security cameras. As usual, her aim was nearly perfect. She missed a few times—firing chocolate-coated rocks with a slingshot isn't easy—but for the most part, she found her targets. The pellets struck the cameras and stuck fast to them, thanks to the adhesive layer of frosting.

Intrigued by the smell, one by one, the bears decided to heck with salmon; it was time for dessert. They abandoned their posts by the fishing stream and shambled into the woods, following the scent of chocolate.

Now that we were close, the size of the Kodiak bears was staggering. They were at least five feet tall while on all fours, with thick, shaggy fur, paws the size of boxing gloves, and six-inch claws. It felt as though we were surrounded by boulders that had suddenly come to life. Whereas black bears scurried through the forest, the Kodiaks lumbered like elephants, trampling anything in their path. They swarmed into the area around Fort King, homing in on the frosting.

Mike was correct to presume there were other warning systems besides the security cameras. I heard the distant whoop of alarms coming from deep inside the fortress, indicating that several hidden sensors had been tripped at once. There were also booby traps, but while these might have worked on puny humans, they had virtually no effect on the bears.

One Kodiak stepped into a noose of rope that was

designed to snap around a person's ankle and trigger a counter-weight to drop from a tree, lifting the victim off the ground and dangling them in the air like a piñata. It didn't budge the bear one inch. Instead, the bear continued onward with the noose around its rear ankle, yanking the counterweight out of the tree and then dragging it along as if it were nothing more than a strand of toilet paper stuck to the bear's foot.

Another trip wire released a several-hundred-pound log hung from a rope, which was supposed to pendulum into an unlucky human with the force of a truck. The bear hardly seemed to notice it. It grunted in annoyance, then lazily swatted the log, which tore free from its suspension and shattered against a rock.

There were plenty of cameras, so each bear had its own to inspect—along with the chocolate affixed to it. Several bears approached the cameras head-on, as we had hoped they would, so that any Russians watching the feeds would see them. Most of the bears ripped the cameras off the trees where they had been mounted, then held them in their massive paws and licked up the frosting—although a few simply bit the cameras off, chewed on them for a bit, and then spit out the parts they didn't like.

Eventually, Russian shouting came from the fortress. It sounded like someone was very annoyed at the bears for ruining a lot of expensive equipment.

Erica instantly leapt into action. Now that all the cameras and booby traps were dismantled—and the bears around us were distracted by chocolate frosting—she raced down the wooded slope toward the fort. Since the old building was constructed directly into the hill, it was easy to access the roof, and she ran right across it, arriving above the front door just as one of the Russian agents burst through it.

The man was angry and armed for combat with a bear. He carried a beanbag gun and wore a bandolier that held a dozen cans of bear repellent. The closest bear to the door was up on its hind legs, trying to pry a security camera off a pine tree. The Russian shouted what I presumed was a nasty comment at the bear, then fired a beanbag to chase it off.

Beanbag guns were generally used to put down criminals or rioters. The beanbags could hit hard enough to incapacitate a human but wouldn't cause any lasting damage. The beanbag had no effect on the bear at all. It simply bounced off the bear's thick hide and plopped to the ground, as though the Russian had shot a battleship. The bear didn't even notice that it had been attacked.

The same could not be said for the Russian agent. While he was busy shooting the bear, Erica leapt onto him from the roof. Even though the man was twice as big as her, Erica had the element of surprise. Within seconds, her opponent was down and unconscious.

Erica took his beanbag gun, his bandolier of bear spray, and his radio.

The rest of us nimbly threaded our way through the gauntlet of bears, then joined Erica at the door to the fort.

The Russian agent had left it open behind him in his hurry to confront the bears.

We cautiously peered inside.

At first, the cabin appeared to be an abandoned relic from the Russian occupation of Alaska. It was small and crudely built, with minimal furnishings coated in a century of dust: a lopsided wooden table, a cast-iron stove, some cobweb-strewn oil lamps. Roots from the trees on the roof poked down through the ceiling like stalactites. However, that was all merely a front to throw off anyone who might have stumbled across it.

The dust on the floor had been disturbed, forming a path leading to the rear of the cabin, where a section of the wall hung slightly ajar, revealing a secret door. The Russian agent had left this open too.

Erica used the barrel of the beanbag gun to pry it open, revealing a passageway.

A tunnel had been blasted through the earth behind the cabin, plunging deeper into the rocky slope that we had just descended. A string of bare light bulbs struggled to illuminate it, but there were still several long, dark stretches.

Distant voices echoed through the gloom. More people speaking Russian.

"They sound angry," Zoe observed warily.

"Russians *always* sound angry," Erica replied, then led the way inside.

I closed the front door to the fort, just to make sure no bears wandered in, then followed the others.

We had only gone a few steps into the tunnel when it forked. Voices came from both directions. One of them belonged to Cyrus. Given the echo in the tunnel, I couldn't tell what he was saying, but he sounded as though he was under duress.

Upon hearing this, Erica's eyes filled with concern. She pointed Zoe and Mike toward the tunnel that Cyrus wasn't in and whispered, "You two go that way. Take care of any trouble. This ought to help." She handed them the bandolier full of bear spray but plucked one of the cans free for me. "This stuff also works on humans. Ben, you're with me." Without waiting for a response, she headed after her grandfather.

Mike and Zoe didn't question the orders. It would have taken time—and made a ruckus. They simply armed themselves with bear spray and headed off into the darkness.

I followed Erica down the other branch. The dimly lit tunnel was dank and dripping with water that had leached in from higher ground. It would have been unnerving to pass through even without knowing that enemy agents were lurking somewhere in it.

It wasn't exactly chivalrous, but I let Erica go ahead of me. If we ran into trouble, she was much better prepared to handle it. She led the way, armed with the beanbag gun and the bear spray, ready for anything that came at her, which was a great system for dealing with any trouble ahead.

But it wasn't so good for sneak attacks from the rear.

Which was what happened.

I'm not sure exactly how a Russian agent got behind us. Perhaps he had emerged from a branch of the tunnel we had missed, or maybe he had arrived at the fort from somewhere else on the island, found it under assault, and raced in to help.

Whatever the case, he got the jump on me. He was a big man, but he moved with such stealth that I never heard him coming. Erica had just rounded a bend in the tunnel, disappearing from my sight. As I was about to follow her, the Russian grabbed me from behind. A meaty hand clamped over my mouth before I could call for help. Arms as thick as pythons wrapped around me, squeezing the air from my lungs. The can of bear spray slipped from my grasp and clattered to the floor.

I hoped Erica would double back to save me, but she was so intent on finding her grandfather, she didn't even seem to notice I was missing.

I was on my own.

SELF-DEFENSE

Fort King

Kodiak Island

July 17

1400 hours

The Russian agent was built like an oak tree. His grasp was so tight, I couldn't breathe. My whole body was in pain, and my mind was getting fuzzy from the lack of oxygen. In another few seconds, I was going to be unconscious.

So I beat him up.

My ability to do this came as a surprise to me.

In my whole time at spy school, I had always been at the bottom of the class in self-defense. But that was because everyone else in spy school was *really* good at fighting. Even as I improved, they improved as well—which obscured the fact that I had been steadily getting better. Over the past few weeks, my self-defense training sessions had intensified, and I was now in excellent physical condition.

It turned out, I was a lean, mean, fighting machine.

I didn't even think about what I was doing. I simply did it.

Since the only parts of my body that I could move were my legs, I performed a Reverse Kneecap Crunch, which startled my attacker into loosening his grip on me. Now that I had a little more freedom, I used my right elbow to make a Mongolian Spleen Jab, then used the Oily Cobra Technique to slip from his grasp. The agent came at me again, but I deftly performed a series of moves called the Sprightly Eye Poke, the Tornado Chest Strike, and the Abrupt Kick to the Soft Bits. The agent stumbled backward, slipped on the can of bear spray I'd dropped, and landed on his back, whacking his head on the stone floor so hard that he was knocked unconscious.

That final move was called Getting Very Lucky, but I wasn't going to question it. Instead, I posed dominantly over my fallen opponent and crowed, "That's what happens when you mess with Ben Ripley!"

"Easy there, Tiger," said Erica.

I wheeled around to find her standing behind me.

Normally, I might have been embarrassed to be caught in the act of preening, but I was too excited by what I had done. "Look!" I exclaimed. "I beat up my first bad guy!"

"I see. It feels pretty good, yes?"

"It's way better than 'pretty good.' It feels amazing!"

"So, do you want to fight some more bad guys?"

"Er . . . no. I think I ought to quit while I'm ahead." I retrieved the can of bear spray, then thought to ask, "Why? Are there more bad guys nearby?"

"There *were*. But they're no longer a problem." Erica led me around the corner of the tunnel.

Four enemy agents were sprawled there, out cold. While I had been defeating one man, Erica had been defeating four times as many.

"Oh," I said, not feeling quite so cool anymore. "Nice work."

"This is why I couldn't come back to help you right away. But you didn't need me, anyhow. You did good." Erica gave me a warm smile, which made me feel even better than I had after beating up my first bad guy.

Beyond the unconscious agents, a thick wooden door blocked the tunnel. There was a relatively new thumbprint scanner built into the lock.

A scream of pain came from the other side of the door. Cyrus.

"Grandpa!" Erica exclaimed, then looked to me. "Help me drag one of these gorillas to the door."

We found the smallest of the unconscious agents, which wasn't saying much; the man still weighed at least two hundred pounds. Together, we lugged him to the scanner, then pressed one of his thumbs to it.

The door clicked open.

Erica and I burst through.

We found ourselves in a large room that had been carved into the rock. It was cold and clammy and not the slightest bit pleasant, which made sense, given that it was basically a hole in the ground. Cyrus was bound to a heavy chair with thick ropes, while another man sat facing him.

The man looked like the FSB version of Cyrus. He appeared to be about the same age, with the same wizened, battle-scarred face, gray-white hair, and unruly eyebrows. They were even dressed alike, in clothes designed for the rugged conditions in Alaska.

I had expected to see a table with implements of torture laid out on it, or a generator with electrodes attached to sensitive spots on Cyrus's body, or possibly even a medieval device like a stretching rack or an iron maiden.

Instead, there was a pot of tea.

It was a rather dainty-looking teapot at that, bone china with a light blue floral design. It was set on a spindly card table between Cyrus and the other man, along with two mugs.

Contrary to what Erica had said earlier, Cyrus *was* having a tea party.

Although he obviously hadn't been enjoying it.

"Erica!" he cried happily upon seeing her. "I knew you'd come!"

Erica seemed just as surprised by the circumstances as I was. "You're not being tortured?"

The other man laughed and then answered before Cyrus could, speaking with a thick Russian accent. "No, my dear. I tortured your grandfather plenty of times over the years—and vice versa—but it never worked. On either end. I was too tough to give him any information—and he was too stubborn to give me any. My government eventually realized that torture is simply not a good way to get information from anyone. Instead, we have been encouraged to try kindness."

Erica looked to her grandfather. "But you just screamed in pain."

"The tea was very hot," Cyrus said meekly. "I burned my tongue."

"Allow me to introduce myself," the Russian man said. "I am—"

"Ivan Ivanovich Shumovsky of the FSB," Erica finished. "And before that, the KGB. My grandfather has told me all about you."

Ivan laughed again. "I suppose that makes sense. And I know all about you from him, Erica Hale. Although you . . ." He looked at me blankly. "I do not know who you are."

"Ben Ripley," I replied. "Cyrus has probably mentioned me."

"No. He has not."

"Are you sure?" I asked, surprised. "Because I've been on several missions with Cyrus. I've even saved the world a few times."

"I'm sure," Ivan said.

"Maybe Cyrus said my name and you misheard it," I suggested. "Perhaps you thought he said something like Sven Ripley? Or Ken Shipley?"

"He only spoke of Erica," Ivan insisted. *"A lot."*

"Oh," I said, feeling a bit left out.

"I said you'd come to rescue me," Cyrus told Erica cheerfully. "And Ivan didn't believe me, the dummy."

Ivan stiffened ever so slightly at the insult. "You are not rescued yet," he reminded Cyrus.

"But you will be soon." Erica came across the room toward Ivan. "I just took out four of your goons . . ."

"And I took out one," I added proudly.

". . . so I don't think a frail old man like you will give me much trouble." Erica tensed to attack.

Suddenly, someone slammed into her, knocking her off her feet. They had surged out of the shadowy recesses of the room so quickly and quietly that Erica was caught completely by surprise. She tumbled to the rocky floor but recovered in an instant. She sprang back to her feet, fists clenched, ready to fight. . . and finally got a good look at her opponent.

Erica gaped in surprise.

So did I.

The attack hadn't come from another hulking, muscle-bound agent. Instead, Erica was facing a teenage girl.

She was lithe and athletic like Erica, with close-cropped hair that was practically white, and she wore a similar form-fitting outfit designed for action—but while Erica's was black and accented with a white utility belt, the girl's outfit was white with a black belt. In a weird way, they looked like opposite halves of a yin-yang symbol.

Ivan chuckled again, although this time, there was a bit of menace in it. "You are not the only one with a granddaughter on this mission," he informed Cyrus. "This is Svetlana. And seeing how easily she got the jump on Erica, it is obvious that she is far more talented."

"That's a load of hooey!" Cyrus snapped. "Erica was obviously only pretending to drop her guard to lure Svetlana out of hiding. And now she's gonna mop the floor with your granddaughter."

"I do not think so," Ivan replied. "I have trained Svetlana in hand-to-hand combat ever since she could walk."

"I've been training Erica ever since she could *crawl*," Cyrus countered.

Erica and Svetlana were now circling each other, sizing each other up before making a move. Both glared menacingly at their opponent, but I had the disturbing sense that Erica wasn't as confident as usual. Despite Cyrus's claim, Svetlana had definitely caught Erica by surprise, and now she looked to be a formidable opponent.

Even though I had just won my first fight against an enemy, I didn't think I'd be much help against Svetlana. Instead, I tried to defuse the situation before it got out of hand.

"Maybe there's no need for violence right now," I said, then looked to Ivan hopefully. "Could you just tell us what you want with Cyrus?"

Ivan considered this, then nodded. "Perhaps. I *was* about to explain what's going on here before you interrupted us."

Neither Erica nor Svetlana dropped their guard. Keeping her eyes locked on Svetlana, Erica spoke to Ivan. "Don't let me stop you. Feel free to explain."

"I need your grandfather's help to find something," Ivan said. "Something that only a member of the Hale family can locate—because one of your ancestors hid it. Augustus Hale."

"Crikey, Ivan!" Cyrus exploded. "You're not starting up with this baloney again!"

"It's not baloney!" Ivan shouted back. "It is fact!" He

turned to face the rest of us. "In 1867, Augustus Hale colluded with the US government to defraud Russia in the purchase of Alaska. The payment was never delivered to Russia. Which means this land was stolen. All three hundred sixty-five million acres of it. The largest land swindle in history!"

"That's a crackpot theory passed down by your dimwit ancestors!" Cyrus retorted. "There is plenty of proof that the purchase was legitimate, right in the US National Archives."

"It was all doctored by Augustus!" Ivan insisted. "My great-great-grandfather witnessed the fraud for himself!"

"Hold on a moment," I said to Ivan, trying to follow everything. "Your family business is also spying? Just like the Hales?"

Ivan snorted in disgust. "The Shumovsky family is *nothing* like the Hales. Because we are honorable people who did not descend from a backstabbing jackal like Augustus."

"My great-great-grandfather was a thousand times more honorable than yours!" Cyrus hollered.

"You won't be saying that when you find the evidence of his deception," Ivan shot back.

"I'm not about to go looking for something that doesn't exist," Cyrus declared.

"Oh, I think you will." The menace had returned to Ivan's voice. "Because if you don't find the proof that your country cheated Russia, then something very bad is going to happen to the state of Alaska."

Erica was concerned enough to pull her gaze away from Svetlana. "What are you going to do?"

Ivan rolled his eyes. "You really think I'm going to tell you? Then you will just focus on thwarting my plan instead of doing what I want you to do, which is finding the evidence."

"How do we know you're not bluffing?" I asked.

"Because I am a man of honor."

"A man of honor who is going to do something terrible to an entire state if we don't meet his demands?" I asked.

Ivan shrugged. "I said I was honorable. I didn't say I was nice."

"What you are is irrational," Cyrus declared. "Just like everyone else in your family. You and I have been over this before. . . ."

"But this time, I have new evidence." Ivan dramatically produced a dossier from his jacket. "I have been combing through my family's own archives—and I came across *this*." He removed an ancient piece of paper from the dossier. It was sealed in a plastic evidence bag to protect it from the elements, which made sense, as it was so old it was practically translucent. "This is a letter from my great-great-grandfather to my great-great-grandmother. I know you can read Russian, Cyrus. So translate what it says right here."

Ivan held the letter in front of Cyrus.

Erica and Svetlana continued to study each other warily, prepared to attack at the slightest provocation.

"'My dearest Irina,'" Cyrus read, "'I am so sorry to hear of the plague that killed all our goats. Perhaps we should sell one of our children to help cover expenses—'"

"Not that part!" Ivan said, looking embarrassed. "This part here!" He pointed to a spot lower down on the letter.

Cyrus dutifully translated that portion. "'The czar has asked me to observe the transfer of funds for Alaska closely—and I believe the reasons for his suspicions are particularly flatulent.'"

"Well-founded," Ivan corrected. "Your translating skills are pathetic."

"This handwriting is what's pathetic," Cyrus replied. "I'm doing my best." He returned his attention to the letter. "'I have caught wind of a deceitful plot called Operation Hornswoggle that may involve my American counterpart in espionage, Augustus Hale, who is a notorious hedgehog—'"

"Scoundrel," Ivan insisted. "Can't you read Russian at all?"

"I can read it just fine," Cyrus snapped. "Your ancestor couldn't *write* it. All his *B*s look like *P*s." He gave the translation one last shot. "'Rest assured, my darling, that I shall investigate this affair thoroughly and discover what fiendish scheme the Americans have planned.'"

Ivan whisked the letter away from him. "This was dated only three days before the transfer of funds for Alaska was supposed to occur. But it never happened—and Augustus was obviously involved!"

"That is a bald-faced lie," Cyrus growled.

"Then feel free to try to prove me wrong," Ivan challenged. "Find out what this Operation Hornswoggle was. Augustus must have left some record of it."

"And what if he didn't?" Cyrus asked pointedly. "Where am I even supposed to look?"

"The CIA has an archive with every recorded mission in the history of the United States," Ivan replied.

"First of all, there was no such mission," Cyrus said. "And even if there was, the archives are sealed. . . ."

"Except for people with the highest levels of access," Ivan continued. "For which you qualify—as both an agent and a descendent of that mangy dog Augustus. Any evidence of Operation Hornswoggle will be there. I want you to find it and bring it to me, so that I can prove once and for all that Alaska is the true property of Russia. Which means that the billions of dollars' worth of oil and gold and other natural resources of this land are rightfully ours."

"This is senseless," Cyrus told him. "You're a madman."

"I am a man who is mad, yes," Ivan agreed. "Very, very mad. And so I think I will use one more thing as leverage to ensure your cooperation in this endeavor." He whipped out a gun and pointed it at Erica. "I am going to hold your granddaughter hostage."

CONFRONTATION

Fort King

Kodiak Island

July 17

1430 hours

Once again, I leapt into action without hesitation.

I still had my can of bear spray.

Like Erica had said, it was also effective on humans.
The can was designed to shoot up to thirty-five feet and to
disperse the pepper in a fog, which was more likely to get in
the nose and eyes of an attacking bear.

I fired the spray at Ivan, temporarily blinding him.

Unfortunately, I also hit Cyrus with the blast, blinding
him as well.

Both men screamed, writhing in pain. Ivan lowered his gun and tried to wipe the pepper from his eyes.

Now that there was no longer a weapon pointed at her, Erica took advantage of the distraction to attack Svetlana.

However, Svetlana was just as prepared. She attacked Erica at the exact same moment.

I had seen Erica face challenging adversaries before, but Svetlana was better than any of them. They seemed to be equals in every form of martial art. Erica would attempt a wushu move, and Svetlana would respond with the perfect counterattack. Then Svetlana would unleash a textbook Nook-Bhan-San technique, which Erica would expertly deflect. It was an amazing display, and my attention probably would have been riveted to it if I hadn't needed to fight for my life.

Despite his age, Ivan was hard as nails. I'd hit him with enough bear spray to fend off a half-ton grizzly, and yet, he refused to go down. His eyes were swollen shut and he was coughing and retching, but he still staggered out of the noxious cloud, waving his gun. "You will pay for this, Ripley!" he roared.

I launched myself at him before he could fire, grabbing the gun and trying to wrest it from his grasp.

Meanwhile, Cyrus was still reeling from the bear spray himself—and he was obviously unhappy with me for catching him with friendly fire. "You hit me, Ripley!" he wheezed.

"I'm blind, you Fort King idiot!" (He didn't exactly say "Fort King," but the word he chose was awfully close.)

Erica and Svetlana continued their battle at one end of the cave, unleashing every move they had against each other. Together, they put on a dazzling display of punches, kicks, jabs, feints, blocks, and responses. At the same time, I was still grappling for the gun with Ivan, who stubbornly refused to succumb to bear spray like a normal person. He was in excellent shape for a man his age and kept a viselike grip on the weapon, no matter what I tried. Even the Abrupt Kick to the Soft Bits didn't work on him. Instead, it backfired against me, as my toe painfully clanged against metal.

"You think I'm an amateur?" he snarled at me. "I'm wearing steel underwear."

"Steel underwear?" I repeated, despite myself. "That must be *very* uncomfortable."

"Yes, but we Russians are much tougher than you." Ivan tried to yank the gun away.

I held on to it, though, and it accidentally discharged, sending a bullet ricocheting off the cave walls.

"Careful, you Fort King morons!" Cyrus screamed. "You're gonna kill someone!" Still bound to the chair, he made a desperate attempt to free himself but only managed to topple the card table, sending the tea service crashing to the floor.

The conflicts might have remained at a stalemate if Mike and Zoe hadn't arrived. They raced into the room and stopped short upon seeing Erica and me fighting the Russians. I heard Zoe gasp with surprise.

My attention was mostly focused on Ivan, but it appeared that Svetlana was startled by the appearance of my friends as well. She dropped her guard for a split second, which was all Erica needed to gain the advantage. She executed a superb Wily Cheetah Leg Sweep, knocking Svetlana to the ground, and then finished her off with a flawless Here Comes the Avalanche move. Svetlana gave a small yelp of pain and then passed out.

Ivan heard her cry and turned her way, dropping his guard as well.

I snatched the gun from his grasp.

Ivan was so concerned about his granddaughter, he barely noticed. "Svetlana!" he yelled, staring blindly into the darkness. "Are you all right?"

"She's fine," Erica replied. "She's just taking a little nap."

"Well *I'm* not so fine!" Cyrus roared. "I've been blinded, and I'm still bound to a chair! Get me out of here!"

Erica staggered to his side to untie him. She was obviously winded and aching from her fight, which indicated how dangerous an opponent Svetlana had been. Normally, Erica could beat up several people at once without breaking a sweat—as she had just done with the Russian guards only minutes before.

"We have to get out of here fast," Mike said. "The sub has returned, and a whole lot of Russians are heading this way from it. I think they know we're here."

Beside him, Zoe was staring at Svetlana's prone body with a faraway look in her eyes. She seemed strangely unsettled by the Russian junior spy.

"There is no point in running," Ivan said, although since he was temporarily sightless, he was facing a wall instead of us. "I may have lost my hostage, but I still have leverage over you."

"You don't have diddly-squat," Cyrus told him. "We don't have to do anything you—whoa!" He stood up as Erica untied the ropes, only to find that his legs had fallen asleep after being tightly bound for so long. He pitched forward and face-planted on the floor.

"You have to do *exactly* what I want," Ivan demanded. "Remember my doomsday plan for Alaska? If you don't get me the information I need in seventy-two hours, I will put that into effect."

"There's a doomsday plan?" Mike asked, stunned. "How much did Zoe and I miss?"

"A lot," I said, backing toward the door. "I'll explain everything as we escape."

"There is no escape!" Ivan roared. "You have no choice! Millions of lives hang in the balance!"

Erica had pulled Cyrus to his feet, but in her exhausted state, she was having trouble helping him to the door. Mike rushed to their aid, and together, all three headed for the tunnel that led out of the fort.

Zoe was still staring at Svetlana. I had to take her by the arm and tell her, "C'mon. We have to go."

Zoe looked to me, startled, as though her mind had been somewhere else. "What's that?"

"We have to go," I repeated, pulling her toward the exit. "What's gotten into you? Are you okay?"

"I'm fine," she said defensively, and in that moment, she sounded like herself again. "Why wouldn't I be fine?"

"Stop the jabbering and move it!" Cyrus ordered.

Zoe and I fell in with the others as they left the room.

Behind us, Ivan continued to yell. "This isn't over! You know how to reach me, Cyrus! If I don't hear from you within three days, Operation Doomsday begins!"

We fled through the rock tunnel. Now that we were moving as fast as we could, rather than stealthily creeping along, the tunnel turned out to be much shorter than I had realized. We were back in the log cabin in less than a minute.

Outside, the bears had finished every last trace of chocolate frosting and gone back to plucking salmon out of the streams.

As Mike had warned, the submarine had returned. Its conning tower poked from the deep water at the far end of the inlet. The sub itself was too big to fit through the narrow waterway, so three Zodiacs full of Russian seamen were heading toward shore. They shouted with surprise upon seeing us.

However, they still had a good distance to go. We raced back up the wooded slope behind Fort King, disappearing into the thick forest.

The Russians fired a few shots after us, but the trees easily covered our escape.

The bears didn't seem to notice.

Cyrus had regained the feeling in his legs and was able to move on his own again, although his eyes were still bleary from the bear spray, so Erica had to guide him. He was obviously embarrassed about being a burden and still cranky after being gassed. "You don't have to hold my arm," he snapped. "I'm not a baby!" He pulled away from Erica and promptly ran straight into a spruce tree.

Erica dutifully returned to his side. Cyrus didn't apologize, but he sullenly let her lead the way once more.

Within five minutes, we reached the top of the slope. Then we ran through the woods for another twenty minutes, putting as much distance between us and the Russians as we could. After that, we had to take a break. Even Erica was panting, while the rest of us were ready to collapse from exhaustion.

We stopped at a jagged outcrop of volcanic rock that poked above the treetops, allowing us to look back the way we had come. In the distance, we could see the cliffs around the inlet, although Fort King was hidden from sight at the bottom. We could also see the smoldering remains of our training helicopter in the bog.

It was a little past three in the afternoon, but since it was summer in Alaska, the sun wasn't going to set until nearly eleven p.m. It was still so high in the sky that it felt like noon in the lower forty-eight states.

Now that we had stopped moving, the mosquitoes attacked in force. Fortunately, repellent was one of the things I kept in my utility belt, and we all promptly slathered it on.

We also dug into our stash of snacks, as we were starving.

Erica studied the woods between us and the inlet, devouring a handful of raisins. "The Russians aren't following us," she observed.

"Of course not," Cyrus replied. "We shook them."

"No, Grandpa. They don't have to follow us. They're probably tending to Ivan and the others instead. Like Ivan said, he has us over a barrel. We have to do what he wants."

Cyrus snorted. "I'm not running off to Langley to search the CIA's classified files for something that doesn't exist. That's a fool's errand. Ivan's a lunatic."

"A lunatic with a doomsday plan. So he's still calling the shots."

"Can someone please explain what's going on here?" Mike asked, exasperated. "Who was that Ivan guy?"

"And who was that girl?" Zoe added.

"Ivan's an old nemesis of mine," Cyrus explained. "The Shumovskys have been causing trouble for the Hales for over two hundred years. He and I had plenty of run-ins back in the old days. He's a good spy—but a nutcase."

"And the girl was his granddaughter, Svetlana," I said.

"Svetlana," Zoe repeated, as though the name had special meaning for her.

Mike gaped at me. "Cyrus's Russian nemesis has a butt-kicking granddaughter too? So she's kind of like Erica's evil twin?"

"She's not *that* good," Erica said, unwittingly touching a bruise on her arm that Svetlana had given her.

"Anyhow," Cyrus went on, "Ivan's had this harebrained theory for years that the United States never actually bought Alaska from Russia. He thinks we made the sale look legit, but then stiffed them when it came time to pay and covered the whole thing up."

Mike whistled appreciatively. "If Russia still owned Alaska, that would shift the geopolitical structure of the entire world. They'd own all those resources . . ."

". . . and a huge piece of North America," Erica added. "Which would allow them to build military bases and missile silos even closer to the rest of the US. Not to mention giving them almost total control of the Arctic Ocean . . ."

"Russia doesn't own Alaska!" Cyrus barked. "Ivan's theory doesn't hold any water!"

"Are you sure?" I asked warily. "He seems awfully convinced it's true."

"A couple weeks ago, millions of people were convinced that you were an alien lizard trying to overthrow the governments of the world," Cyrus reminded me. "And they were obviously wrong. Blind faith in something doesn't make it real."

He was referring to Murray Hill's most recent plan, where he had spread conspiracy theories about all of us online—only to have actual conspiracy theorists add to them, making them wilder and wilder. Even though our government had done its best to discredit the lies, a great number of people still believed them, which was part of the reason we had relocated to such a remote area to train; it was still unsafe for us to be around the general population.

"Good point," I admitted.

Cyrus said, "The sale of Alaska went exactly as it was negotiated between the US and Russia in 1867. There's plenty of documentation in the National Archives to prove it. I've personally examined the check for the purchase."

"Hold on," Mike said. "The United States paid for Alaska with a check? That seems suspicious."

"The check was ceremonial," Cyrus explained. "Kind of like one of those big ones they give sweepstakes winners. But it was issued as proof of the sale. The actual payment of seven point two million dollars in gold was made in Washington, where Secretary of State Seward handed it off to Russian Minister Edouard de Stoeckl with great fanfare. There were plenty of witnesses, including Augustus Hale. There's no evidence of any hanky-panky at all."

"Although Ivan certainly seems to think there is," Erica told her grandfather. "He had the letter. . . ."

"Which was just more Shumovsky family lunacy," Cyrus said dismissively. "There was never any Operation Hornswoggle. That's a load of bunk."

Mike made a sudden gasp of surprise.

Erica ignored this and asked her grandfather, "Do you think there's a way we can prove that? Some sort of documentation in the CIA archives?"

"Even if there was, Ivan wouldn't believe it," Cyrus replied. "Flying all the way to Washington to comb through the archives would be a colossal waste of time. What we need to do is stay here, figure out what Ivan's doomsday scheme is, and thwart it before that clown gets a chance to put it in action."

"Actually," Mike said, "there *might* be some information about Operation Hornswoggle back in Washington, DC. But it won't be in the CIA archives."

We all turned to him, surprised by this comment. Mike looked rather startled himself. Like he couldn't quite believe what he was saying.

"Why's that?" Cyrus demanded.

"Because Hornswoggle wasn't a CIA operation," Mike replied. "It was the Croatoan's."

CONSPIRACY

Kodiak Island, Alaska
July 17
1530 hours

The Croatoan was an evil organization that my friends and I had confronted a few months earlier. It had originally been formed by the Spanish back in the early 1600s to contest Britain's attempts to colonize North America, but once the United States declared its independence, the Croatoan had shifted its focus. A sect of the organization had worked in the shadows of history, doing everything it could to undermine the USA.

"Remember when we found their secret headquarters?"

Mike asked. "And there were all those filing cabinets full of evil plans that they had concocted?"

"Yes," Erica and I said at once, although Zoe made a small groan in response. At the time, the Croatoan had made Erica appear to be a double agent, and while Mike and I had refused to believe she'd switched sides, Zoe had—which had driven a wedge into our friendship for a while. So Zoe hadn't been with us when we'd found the Croatoan's headquarters.

The files Mike was referring to had detailed all of the organization's plots over several hundred years, showing that the group had been involved behind the scenes in just about every bad event in American history, from the Civil War to the Great Depression to the 1990s fashion craze for neon-colored parachute pants.

"Well," Mike went on, "there was a file in there about something called Operation Hornswoggle back in the 1860s."

"Are you sure?" Erica questioned.

"Definitely," Mike assured her. "You don't forget a name like Operation Hornswoggle."

"And what did the file say?" I asked.

Mike grimaced. "I don't know. I didn't read it."

"What?" Cyrus exploded. "Why the heck not?"

"Because there were *hundreds* of files," Mike explained.

"There wasn't time to read them all. I was busy looking at the ones about pirates and the stock market crash and the Boston Tea Party. And then the Croatoan showed up and we had to run away."

Cyrus still looked ready to lash into Mike for failing to read the file, but Erica cut him off before he could. "That's a valid excuse. No one could have gone through all those files in the brief time we had."

"And, unfortunately, we'll never get the chance to see them again," I added. "After the Croatoan chased us off, they burned down their headquarters and destroyed everything inside."

"Well, that's what they *wanted* us to think, at least," Erica said.

"Oh!" Mike exclaimed. "Do you suppose they moved the files before torching the place?"

"It's possible," Erica replied.

"Although it's equally possible that they didn't," Cyrus groused.

Erica suddenly cocked her head, as if she had heard something. As usual, her senses were so well attuned that she picked up on the sound before the rest of us did, although it was only a few seconds before I heard it too: a faint whirring. Kodiak Island was so remote and devoid of civilization that it was eerily quiet, so we could hear the noise from a great distance away. I looked off toward the horizon. A tiny speck was moving over the ocean, rapidly coming our way.

"Is that Alexander and Catherine?" Zoe asked, sounding relieved.

"I told you I was going to call them," Erica reported. "I sent them a message from our camp before we left. They're homing in on a signal from my phone. We need to get to flat ground." She quickly started downhill from our perch on the outcrop, heading toward another bog. It looked goopy and mosquito-infested, but since it was flat and devoid of trees, it was the only place nearby where a helicopter could land.

The rest of us followed. Even though we hadn't rested for long, Erica appeared to have fully recovered her stamina. She was obviously still injured—her arms were mottled with bruises—but she showed no sign of being in pain, making her way down the rocky slope so briskly it was a struggle to keep up with her.

I said, "Even if the Croatoan's files *were* destroyed, there's still a way to find out what Operation Hornswoggle was."

"El Capitan," Mike concluded.

"Right," I agreed. El Capitan was the leader of the Croatoan, who we had helped capture after thwarting her plans. "I'm sure she knows about every operation the Croatoan ran throughout its history."

"There's no guarantee of that," Cyrus proclaimed. "Or

that she'd tell us anything. And she's incarcerated in a federal penitentiary back in Virginia. It'll take days to get there, interrogate her, and get back. That time would still be better spent determining what Ivan's doomsday plan is."

"Maybe we could split up," Zoe suggested. "One team could go to Virginia, while the other stays in Alaska."

"Sending any of you to Virginia would be risky," Cyrus cautioned. "Every nutjob in the lower forty-eight still thinks you're a bunch of giant lizards."

"Is it any riskier than staying here?" Mike asked. "We've got the Russians to contend with. And bears. And moose!"

"Moose aren't that dangerous," Zoe said.

"Yes, but we're about to run into one," Mike informed us.

Sure enough, a moose was passing through the woods ahead of us. It was a large bull, with antlers as wide as a refrigerator.

Even though moose were herbivores, they could be just as deadly as a bear. They were big and powerful, and if one felt threatened by you, it could do a lot of damage with its heavy antlers or its sharp hooves. So we all froze in our tracks.

The moose froze as well and regarded us curiously; there was a decent chance that, on this remote part of the island, it had never seen humans before. However, it seemed far more concerned about the approaching helicopter, which was growing louder by the second. After a few moments, the moose trotted off and vanished into the woods with startling ease for an animal that was so large.

We had reached the base of the outcrop, and the bog lay just ahead. We hurried through the forest and emerged into the open space. It was even soggier than the bog we had crash-landed in earlier. Oozing mud sucked at our muck boots as we squelched across it.

The helicopter arrived, roaring over the treetops, and then came to an abrupt stop, close enough that I could see Alexander and Catherine Hale waving from the cockpit. The chopper was a vintage Russian military transport that had been given to Alexander by an exceptionally wealthy computer programmer who couldn't recall why he'd even bought it in the first place. It wasn't fancy, but it was still far better than the trainer; at the very least, it could go long distances without falling apart.

Alexander slowly lowered the helicopter and hovered just above the bog, possibly fearing that if he landed, the heavy craft would sink into the mud and get stuck there. The wind from the rotors kicked up plenty of gunk, which pelted us wetly. But it also blew the mosquitoes away, which was nice.

We made our way to the helicopter as fast as we could, which wasn't really that fast at all, since it was hard to run across the soupy bog. Catherine flung open the side doors of the helicopter, and we piled inside, one by one.

Mike and I brought up the rear. As I reached the chopper, something glinted in the forest at the edge of the bog, as though light had reflected off a piece of glass. Fearing it might be a Russian sniper's sight, I hurriedly leapt aboard. Mike was right behind me, and the moment Catherine slammed the door shut, we lifted back into the air.

The interior of the helicopter was narrow with a line of jump seats along each wall. Much of the remaining space was filled with the supplies Alexander and Catherine had amassed on their run to civilization: crates of canned food, sacks of rice and beans, bales of toilet paper, canisters of butane.

"Sorry it's so cramped," Catherine apologized. She was British and worked for MI6, their intelligence service. She was an excellent spy and a doting mother; in her capable hands, a simple skillet could be used to either whip up a world-class meal or knock out a few bad guys. She also had the most delightful lilt to her voice. "We had just finished shopping when we got your emergency message, and we didn't want to waste time stopping at camp to unload."

Rather than taking a jump seat, I peered out the window as we rose from the bog, staring at the spot where I had seen the flash of light. The woods were thick, but I thought I caught a glimpse of white material deep in the shadows.

"Svetlana," Erica said. She was standing beside me but

not looking out the window at all. She didn't need to. She must have already spotted her rival.

"What do you think she's doing?" I asked, wondering if I should be concerned.

"Only observing us. She had a pair of binoculars. But no weapon that I could see."

That explained the glint of light; it was the sun reflecting off the binocular lenses.

"Was she alone?" I asked.

"As far as I could tell."

The forest quickly dropped away below us, and as we rose, I could see the inlet where Fort King was located. From our height, the oblong outline of the Russian submarine was evident in the ocean beyond it.

"What's our heading?" Alexander asked.

"That's still a matter of debate," Cyrus replied, and then told them everything that had happened. While he spoke, Alexander flew in the opposite direction from Fort King, rapidly putting distance between us and the Russians. The green trees and rocky peaks of Kodiak Island sped below us in a blur.

". . . which is why we have to stay close by and figure out what the Russians are plotting," Cyrus concluded.

"Ivan said he'd call off Operation Doomsday if we got him the information he wanted," Mike reminded him.

"I don't trust Ivan one bit," Cyrus grumped.

"It's still worth a shot," Erica argued. "At least some of us should head to Virginia to find out what El Capitan knows about Operation Hornswoggle."

"That's a waste of time and resources," Cyrus insisted.

"Pardon the interruption," Catherine said, looking very apologetic, "but I think there's a way to learn about Operation Hornswoggle without going all the way to Virginia. There's a person who might know about it right here in Alaska."

This was news to everyone else in the helicopter except Alexander. Even Erica was caught by surprise. "Who?" she asked.

"Murray Hill," Catherine replied.

EXILE

Crooked Island

Off the western coast of Alaska

July 17

2130 hours

I was *tremendously* upset to learn that Murray
Hill was not in prison. After all, he had made me the target
of assassins, placed my friends and me at the center of a massive conspiracy theory, and engineered the destruction of the
main campus of spy school, forcing us to decamp to Alaska.
And that was all just in the last few weeks.

Even more aggravating was the fact that Murray should
have been in jail when he had done all this. Earlier that year,
my friends and I had arrested him for multiple illegal acts,

and then Cyrus had delivered him to the Falcon Ridge federal supermax penitentiary. However, unknown to us, Murray had quickly cut a deal with our own government, trading information about his previous associates in return for a place in the Federal Witness Protection Program. All of this had worked out like a charm for Murray, who got even with his enemies, avoided jail—and was allowed to move into a nice suburban community with a swimming pool. He had then promptly violated all the terms of his release by committing several crimes at once, almost all of which were against me.

After an exceptionally harrowing adventure, my friends and I had recaptured Murray, and afterward, I had expected he would be sent back to jail, hopefully for the rest of his life. So it was a shock to hear that he had managed to weasel out of prison once again.

"There were issues with sending him back," Catherine explained. "He had a legally binding agreement with the Federal Witness Protection Program, and even though he had violated that, in giving up information on his enemies, he had made those same enemies very upset. If he had returned to prison, it wouldn't have been long until someone killed him."

"So?" I asked. It was a callous response, but then, Murray had actively sent professional assassins after me. I didn't have much sympathy for his predicament.

"Civilized governments generally frown on killing," Catherine chided.

"Unless they're at war," Mike pointed out. "Then they're generally really in favor of killing."

"Er . . . yes." Catherine gave a pained expression. "The point is, Murray needed to stay in the Witness Protection Program. But everyone agreed that he still ought to suffer some sort of punishment for his crimes. So Alexander came up with quite a clever solution."

"Alexander?" I repeated, failing to conceal my surprise. The words "Alexander" and "clever" were rarely used in the same sentence—unless there was a "not" in between them somewhere.

"Yes, Alexander," Catherine said. "He knew the perfect place to send Murray."

I sincerely doubted this.

Until I saw it for myself.

I had to admit, I was impressed.

To begin with, Crooked Island was about as remote as you could get and still be in the United States. Even in our helicopter, which was one of the fastest ways to travel around Alaska, it took us six hours to get there.

Crooked Island was an ugly, nearly barren lump of rock that jutted out of a churning sea. It was about a mile across and three miles long, and it was constantly battered by gale-force winds, which left the few trees that managed to grow there stunted and bent nearly flat to the ground. Most of the coastline was steep cliffs that were perpetually pummeled by brutal waves, and the single beach, unlike beaches in tropical climates, was awful. The dismal stretch of coal-black volcanic sand was blustery and frigid. Even though humans had been living in Alaska for thousands of years, every single one of them had decided to avoid Crooked Island. The only habitation on it was a small, lopsided Quonset hut left over from a brief period when munitions had been stored there during World War II.

However, walruses seemed to love the place.

Thousands of them were hauled out on the beach, a writhing, churning mass of blubbery pinnipeds, each of which weighed nearly two tons.

The more I saw of Crooked Island, the happier I became. If I had set out to create a place specifically designed to make Murray Hill miserable, it would have looked exactly like Crooked Island. The place was devoid of all the creature comforts he craved and filled with everything he loathed. Like nature. Murray had once described nature as "the miserable place you have to pass through to get from one air-conditioned building to another." Now he was surrounded by it. Plus, he'd always had an unusual aversion to walruses. Back before I had learned he was evil, when he was posing as a normal, friendly fellow student, he had confided in me that walruses gave him the creeps. I had assured him that there was zero chance of him ending up anywhere near walruses for any length of time, which I was now pleased to discover was entirely wrong.

The sun still hadn't gone down when we arrived, even though it was well past dinnertime. (Thanks to the Hales' supply run, we'd had plenty of food to eat en route.) The sky was gray, as was the ocean. The entire landscape was bleak and dull.

Because of the walruses, the helicopter couldn't land on the beach. Instead, Alexander had to set it down on a corrugated patch of rock on a small rise near the Quonset hut. We all hopped out right away, eager for fresh air, a chance to stretch our legs, and some peace and quiet after the long, noisy flight.

We only got one of the three.

Despite its remoteness, Crooked Island wasn't quiet at all. The wind was howling, the surf was crashing, and—it turned out—walruses are not tranquil creatures. They make a startling variety of noises, although not a single one could be considered melodious. The air was filled with a cacophony of snorts, snuffles, grunts, roars, surprisingly high-pitched whistles, and a bizarre clacking that sounded rather like the helicopter—as well as the belches and blasts of air escaping from various parts of the walruses' bodies, some of which were staggeringly loud.

That meant we didn't have much fresh air, either. Instead, the entire island reeked of walrus gas, which smells like rotten shellfish.

I actually found myself thinking that this place was too awful even for Murray Hill.

We hurried across the sterile, windy landscape, circumvented a few dozing walruses that had hauled themselves up well away from the waterline, and rapped on the door of the Quonset hut.

There was no lock on the door, indicating that Murray was free to come and go as he wished. The island itself was a prison.

I would have expected that the whirr of the helicopter's rotors would have tipped Murray off that someone had arrived, but it seemed that he hadn't heard us over the wind and the surf and the walrus noises. It took him a while to answer the door.

I realized I was on edge. I never knew how Murray would behave each time he saw me. Sometimes, he pretended to be friendly; others, he made no secret of his hatred for me. I wasn't sure which was worse.

Finally, the door opened. The last time I had seen Murray, he had been slovenly and out of shape, the result of a sedentary lifestyle and a diet that was almost exclusively junk food. Now, even though it was only a month later, he looked like an entirely different person. Despite the several layers of clothing he was wearing to stay warm, I could see that he was trim and fit. However, his hair was long and unkempt, his cheeks were covered with fuzzy adolescent whiskers, and his nose was red and swollen. I had seen Murray transform while incarcerated before, but still, the rate at which it happened was startling.

Murray gaped at all of us in shock, stunned by our presence on his doorstep. And then he gave a cry of delight. "Hello, everyone!" he exclaimed. "It's so good to see you! Please come in!"

"You're not upset to see us?" I asked.

"Oh, I definitely am," Murray replied. "I hate all of you very much. But I'm so lonely out here, I'm desperate to see *anyone.* ACHOO!" He blew his nose wetly into a handkerchief. "Sorry. I'm allergic to something on this island. One of the plants . . . or possibly walrus dander." He stepped aside and waved us into the hut.

There wasn't much to it: a small kitchenette with a hot plate and a mini fridge, a cot, a table, two chairs, and several crates full of paperback books. (There was no bathroom inside. Instead, I had noticed an outhouse located down the beach.) A cast-iron stove in the center radiated heat, making the place warm—if not quite cozy. Everything was neat and tidy, which caught us all by surprise.

Zoe noted it first. "Murray, this place is . . . well . . . it's not a pigsty."

"There's not much to do here except tend house." Murray gave her a long, lovelorn look. "By the way, when I said

I hated everyone, I didn't mean *you*. It's wonderful to see you, Zoe. You're looking lovely today." He snatched away a chair that Cyrus was about to sit in and proffered it to Zoe. "Please, make yourself comfortable."

"Thanks very much," Zoe said as sweetly as she could.

This was difficult for her, as she loathed Murray. However, on the way to Crooked Island, Catherine had ordered her to not let Murray know this. We needed information from him, and the best way to get it would be to avoid antagonizing him. If necessary, Zoe was under direct orders to act smitten.

"Would all of you like some tea?" Murray asked. "I brew it myself from plants on the island. I've become quite knowledgeable about the local flora, given that I have virtually nothing else to do with my time." While he tried to sound cheerful about this, he spoke through gritted teeth, indicating that he was struggling to control his rage at all of us.

"Oh!" Catherine said. "A spot of tea would be lovely!" I was quite sure that she wasn't pretending to be nice. She was truly excited about the tea.

The rest of us agreed to it as well, trying to be pleasant.

"Great!" Murray said. "I've already got a kettle on! ACHOO!" He blew his nose again, then hurried to his single kitchen cabinet and began taking out a random assortment of cups and saucers.

Cyrus plunked himself into the one other chair Murray

owned while the rest of us remained standing. There was barely enough room in the hut for the eight of us.

We all looked to Zoe expectantly. As the object of Murray's affection, it seemed that she ought to bring up the reason we were there.

"Murray," she began cautiously, "we were hoping that you could help us with a case that we're working on."

Murray paused in the midst of taking out glassware. "This isn't just a social call?"

"Er . . . not entirely," Zoe admitted.

"So . . . after condemning me to live out here on this godforsaken rock in the middle of nowhere, you weren't coming to check up on me and see how I'm doing? ACHOO! You're only here because you need a favor?"

"Of course we care how you're doing," Zoe said earnestly. She did a good job of selling this, even though I knew it was a struggle for her. "We care about you very much."

"Really? Because you have a funny way of showing it." Murray's anger was beginning to seep through his joy at seeing us. "I mean, look at this horrible place you've banished me to! There's no internet. No TV. Not even a radio. This is the middle of summer, and it's forty-five degrees! And don't get me started on the mosquitoes! Look at me!" He rolled up a sleeve to reveal that his arm was a minefield of little red welts. "I've been bitten so many times, I look like a walking raspberry!"

"It's still better than prison," Mike pointed out.

"Is it?" Murray asked. "At least in prison we got doughnuts on occasion. The closest doughnut shop is nearly a thousand miles from here, and they don't even have sprinkles! There's no junk food at all! No chips! No candy! No *bacon*! I'm living off canned goods and peat moss! There's nothing here but rocks, wind, and walri!"

"Walri?" we all asked, confused.

"Walri," Murray repeated. "It's the plural of 'walrus.' That's how you pluralize words that end in *u-s*, right? Radius, radii. Cactus, cacti. Platypus, platypi."

"But 'walrus' is an exception," Catherine said.

"Like 'circus,'" Mike added. "The plural of 'circus' isn't 'circi.'"

"I'm the one stuck on an island with four thousand walri!" Murray snapped. "Not you! I think *I* should get to decide how to pluralize them! ACHOO!"

"If you say so," Zoe agreed gamely. "I *like* 'walri.'"

"Well I don't," Murray grumbled. "They're the worst. Did you hear them out there? Did you *smell* them? It's not enough that they're bloated and ugly and loud. They have to be flatulent, too? This island is the world capital of walrus farts."

"What if we sent you some air freshener?" Alexander suggested helpfully. "Would that make things better?"

"Do they make cans of air freshener the size of the

Empire State Building?" Murray asked. "Because that's what I'd need to counteract all that stink out there." He lifted a whistling kettle off the hot plate and poured steaming water into the motley assortment of mugs he'd assembled.

Zoe made another attempt to get back to the mission. She fluttered her eyelashes flirtatiously and cooed, "Murray, we need to know about Operation Hornswoggle."

Murray appeared to have been caught by surprise. "*That's* what you're here about?"

"You know what it is?" Mike asked, excited.

"Of course I know what it is." Murray set a warm mug of tea in front of Catherine. "I know lots of stuff. ACHOO! I'm very smart."

"You *are*," Zoe said, like she was impressed. "You're one of the smartest people I've ever met. And it would mean a great deal to me if you could tell us what Operation Hornswoggle was."

Murray set another mug of tea in front of her. He looked very conflicted. Like he really didn't want to help us, but he also didn't want to say no to anything Zoe had asked. After a brief internal struggle, he somehow found the strength to refuse her. "You know what would mean a great deal to me? Getting off this island. So how about we make a deal? I give you the information you want—and you move me someplace that's warm and quiet and walrus-free. Like Hawaii."

"Here's another option," Cyrus growled. "You give us the information we need, and in return, I won't rip your nose off and stick it up your—"

"Cyrus!" Catherine said sharply. "We do not extract information via torture!"

Cyrus sighed heavily. "Fine." Then he muttered under his breath, "Spoilsport."

Catherine returned her attention to Murray while blowing on her tea to cool it. "Moving you any place but here is not an option."

"Then I refuse to help." Murray handed out more steaming mugs. "Although if you'd like to play a board game, I'd be happy to do that. I've had to play Parcheesi against myself for the past few weeks. It's no fun at all."

"How about this?" Mike suggested. "You give us the information—in return for a kiss from Zoe."

"Really?" Murray asked, unable to control his excitement.

"What?" Zoe asked at the exact same time, unable to control her disgust.

"Just a peck on the cheek," Mike amended quickly, then gave Zoe an imploring look. "The fate of millions of people may depend on this."

Zoe grimaced, weighing the benefits of averting a major disaster with having to kiss Murray Hill.

Murray looked to Zoe expectantly. "I'm willing to make

that deal. Are you?" He honked his nose into his handkerchief, which was now sopping with snot.

"Ummm," Zoe replied.

Mike started to say something else, but before he could, I joined them and whispered, "I don't think it's right to put Zoe in this position. If she doesn't want to kiss Murray, then—"

"She's *not* going to kiss Murray," Mike whispered back. "All she has to do is *say* she will. Then he coughs up the information. When the time comes for the smooch, we tell him to close his eyes and pucker up—and then we shove a nice fresh walrus poop in his face and beat it for the helicopter."

Zoe was obviously pleased to hear Mike's *real* plan, although she faked a resigned expression before turning back to Murray. "Okay. I'll kiss you. *After* you give us the information."

"Deal!" Murray crowed.

Catherine smiled. "All right, Murray. Let's hear what you've got." She blew across her tea once more, realized it was cool enough to drink, then lifted the mug to her lips . . .

Only to have Erica slap her hand over it. "Not so fast, Mom. Murray just tried to poison you."

INFORMATION

Crooked Island, Alaska

July 17

2200 hours

"Poison?" Murray asked, acting as though his honor had been questioned. "How could I possibly arrange that? I have no access to anything poisonous out here."

"Except plants," Erica replied. "You said it yourself: You've become an expert on the flora of this island. And one of the plants that grows here is Aleutian gooseberry, a low-lying shrub with leaves that, when ground, create a colorless and *almost* odorless neurotoxin. You need to grind a lot of gooseberry leaves to make it, but you have plenty of time on your hands. I assume you must have already had some prepared, just in case an opportunity like this presented itself. The moment you saw the helicopter coming, you went to work setting the stage to poison us all."

"I would never do something like that!" Murray proclaimed.

Erica plopped a metal spoon into her mother's tea, which sizzled and smoked in response. When Erica removed the spoon, it was partially dissolved, as though it had been dipped in battery acid. "That looks awfully deadly to me."

Murray grinned weakly. "Can't blame a guy for trying, right?"

Catherine set her tea down firmly and gave Murray a withering glare. "On the contrary, I am *very* disappointed in you. In fact, I'm tempted to rescind Zoe's offer to kiss you in return for that information and allow Cyrus to torture you instead."

Cyrus eagerly snapped to his feet. "Sounds good to me."

Murray gave a squeak of alarm. "Okay. I apologize for trying to kill you. I'm very sorry! That was remarkably poor manners of me! But in my defense, I was delirious. Too much walrus gas can addle your brain. Is that kiss still on the table?"

Cyrus cracked his knuckles. "Start talking—or I'm gonna start hurting."

"All right!" Murray yelped. "As you know, I—"

"Sorry to interrupt," Alexander said. "I'm still a bit unclear on the attempted poisoning. Did you put Aleutian gooseberry in everyone's tea, or just my wife's?"

"Everyone's," Murray replied.

"Ah." Alexander inspected his cup carefully. "So then, I shouldn't drink this?"

"No, Dad." Erica took the tea from him and dumped it into the sink, where it smoldered noxiously. Then she looked back at Murray. "Keep talking."

"Sure thing. ACHOO!" Murray mopped his nose with his soggy handkerchief. "As I was saying, I did some freelance work for the Croatoan before you thwarted their plans. So I got to know the gang there. Their whole grudge against the United States was a little obsessive, but still, they were nice folks. They had me over to the secret lair a few times and told me about a couple of their evil schemes. El Capitan *loved* bragging about schemes."

"Look who's talking," Mike whispered to me.

Nobody liked bragging about their own schemes more than Murray Hill. Murray loved to talk, and his favorite subject was how clever he was. Although he now seemed very excited to share how clever the Croatoan were as well. "Operation Hornswoggle was one of El Capitan's favorites. It didn't quite work out the way the Croatoan had hoped, but they still did well from it. Back in 1867, their agents got wind of the Alaska deal and hatched a scheme to mess it up. First, they ran a disinformation campaign to convince the Russians that the US was plotting to swindle them. There was a Russian agent named Schmoopy or something like that—"

"Shumovsky," Cyrus corrected.

"Right. Shumovsky. He totally took the bait. Throughout the entire purchase, he was on guard, waiting for the Americans to try something. But of course, they didn't. The purchase went off exactly as it was supposed to. The Americans handed seven point two million dollars' worth of gold over to the Russians."

"Um . . . ," Mike said. "The Croatoan's plan was to let the purchase go ahead? That doesn't seem very devious."

"The devious part is what the Croatoan did *next*," Murray explained. "Once everyone was assured that the deal had gone down properly, they robbed the Russians."

"They stole all seven point two million dollars?" Catherine asked.

"Every last penny. ACHOO!" Murray honked his nose again. "The Croatoan waited for the Russians to return to their hotel and then ambushed them. They caught Stanislavsky and his team with their pants down."

"Shumovsky," Cyrus corrected once more.

"Right. Shumovsky. Now, here's where the story gets interesting: The Croatoan expected that the Russians would think the Americans were behind the theft, then accuse them of defaulting on the Alaska deal, and maybe they'd end up going to war over the whole thing. But the Russians didn't do that. Instead, they covered up the entire affair."

"Why?" I asked.

"No one's exactly sure. It's possible that they realized the Americans weren't behind the theft—or maybe they simply didn't want to go to war. Russia had just finished fighting the Crimean War, which had been very expensive and deadly, and no one was in the mood to start that up again. But personally, I think the *real* reason for the cover-up was that they were embarrassed about the robbery. I mean, it's bad enough to get mugged and lose your wallet—but to lose seven point two million dollars? That's tremendously humiliating. Obviously, it was a huge intelligence failure for the Russians and Spitonsky."

"You're not even *trying* to get the name right, are you?" Cyrus griped.

"So Russia just ate the loss of all that money?" Zoe asked.

"I guess so. ACHOO! Or maybe, the money was insured against theft. The upshot is, America got Alaska, Russia got screwed . . . and the Croatoan got rich. They had millions to fund future schemes against America, so they didn't really care too much that Operation Hornswoggle hadn't gone exactly as they'd hoped."

"Then Ivan's got this totally wrong," Erica said. "America

paid for Alaska fair and square. His ancestor is the one who botched the deal."

"Well, the Croatoan helped," I said.

"Sure," Cyrus agreed, "but if Shumovsky had been a halfway decent spy, he should have seen that coming. Instead, he allowed himself to be hoodwinked and lost a staggering amount of gold." He burst into laughter. "I can't wait to see the look on Ivan's face when he hears the truth!"

"It's also possible that Shumovsky was in league with the Croatoan," Catherine suggested. "Maybe he got a cut of the money."

"That's even better!" Cyrus crowed happily. "Ivan's beloved ancestor might have been a traitor to his country! This is going to devastate him!"

Despite Cyrus's glee, I still had a sense of concern. It seemed to me that something wasn't quite right during our conversation, although I couldn't grasp what it was. In fact, the more I thought about the entire situation, the fuzzier everything seemed to be. My mind didn't seem to be working as well as usual—and things were getting worse by the second.

Cyrus was still laughing heartily. "As soon as we get back to a place with phone reception, I'm gonna call Ivan right up and tell him to flargleblarrgh." He frowned, looking disturbed that his sentence hadn't finished the way he had intended, then tried to speak again. Only this time, it all came out as gibberish. "Blurgledurgle. Plimterplop. Ska-doobadeeble."

Erica looked at him, worried, and said, "Forgeedorfle?" Then she gasped in fright, aware that she couldn't speak either.

Around the Quonset hut, my friends were all realizing that something was wrong with them. They looked as dis-combobulated as I felt. Even Alexander seemed more con-fused than usual. Everyone was trying to talk but unable to make any sense.

"Freem!" Mike exclaimed.

"Skipperdeedoo!" Zoe cried.

"Flugelhorn!" Alexander shouted.

I pointed accusingly at Murray and screamed, "Plurrupta bumbding!" Which was a desperate attempt to say "You're up to something."

A knowing grin spread across Murray's face. "Ah. It seems the sedative I've given you has kicked in."

Erica, Cyrus, and Catherine all tried to attack him at once, but none of them could make their bodies do what they wanted. Instead, Erica and Catherine merely staggered in circles, while Cyrus tumbled backward into his chair.

My own arms and legs suddenly felt as though they each weighed a hundred pounds. I couldn't move them. Instead, they were dragging me toward the floor.

Meanwhile, Murray was completely immune to whatever was affecting us. He gleefully explained his evil scheme. "As we've established, I have come to know the local plants here quite well. And there are other dangerous ones besides the Aleutian gooseberry—which I only put in your tea to distract you from my *real* plan. I figured Erica would expect me to try something dastardly—but that once she'd thwarted my attempts to poison you, she'd let her guard down."

"Frimmina flimflum!" Erica shouted angrily. She was still struggling to get to Murray, but her limbs obviously wouldn't do what she wanted them to. Instead, her knees buckled, and she fell into a sitting position on the floor.

The same thing then happened to me. And Mike. And Catherine. And Alexander. Since Zoe and Cyrus were already seated, they merely sagged in their chairs.

Murray pointed to the cast-iron stove in the center of the hut. "In addition to the logs in there, I added a few handfuls of Siberian snodgrass. The smoke from it is a powerful tranquilizer."

"Buddiderrenchoo splimntected?" Mike demanded.

"Why wasn't I affected?" Murray translated tauntingly. "A very good question. The antidote to Siberian snodgrass also grows here: arctic bungweed. I ground a bit of that up and concealed it here." He proudly held up the damp handkerchief he'd been blowing his nose into since we'd arrived.

"I haven't had to sneeze at all! That was just an excuse to keep from inhaling the snodgrass. Although I do think I've gotten hives from the walrus dander. But that's no longer my problem, thanks to you suckers."

"Baloo babbadorking!" Cyrus yelled angrily, and then passed out, face-first, onto the table.

Nearby, Catherine and Alexander both slumped to the floor and began snoring.

Murray calmly rifled through Alexander's pockets until he found the keys to the helicopter.

My friends and I watched helplessly. I couldn't even feel my arms and legs now, let alone control them. And my head felt like someone had removed my brain and filled my skull with cotton candy.

Murray stopped before me and dangled the keys in front of my nose. "I've been plotting how to escape this dump ever since I got here. I figured I'd have to maroon some poor sap and then seek my revenge on you—but I never dreamed that I'd get to do both at the same time." He burst into joyful laughter.

"Mummydum snarkleblast," Zoe growled at him angrily.

Murray stopped laughing and turned to her, looking genuinely sympathetic. "I don't have to leave *you* here, my darling. Just say the word, and I'll fly us away to someplace warm and romantic."

If Zoe had been thinking properly, she would have played along. She would have nodded and made goo-goo eyes at Murray, tricking him into taking her with him. Then once she had her strength back, she could have overwhelmed him and sent help for us.

But in her addled state, she couldn't control her true emotions. She made a face of disgust and said "Bleccch." I wasn't sure whether she was actually trying to say that—or if she had been trying to say something more erudite and "bleccch" was what had come out instead—but either way, it certainly got the point across.

Murray recoiled, his feelings obviously hurt. "Ah. I see. Given the choice between me or exile on an island full of farting walri . . . you're picking the walri. Very well. Have a nice life." He stormed out of the hut, leaving the door wide open.

This allowed a frigid wind inside, along with plenty of toxic walrus gas.

It was finally getting somewhat dark, but I could still see Murray as he headed down to the helicopter and started the engines.

The last thing I witnessed, before the Siberian snodgrass finally overwhelmed me and knocked me out, was the chopper lifting off, stranding us on Crooked Island.

DESPERATION

Crooked Island
July 18
0900 hours

Siberian snodgrass must be an exceptionally powerful sedative, because I slept soundly for the next ten hours, despite lying on the hard floor of a frigid Quonset hut with the din of a raging wind and gassy walruses outside. (Of course, I'd had an exceptionally exhausting day, so it's possible that I would have slept that long even without being knocked out.)

When I finally regained consciousness, I was able to move my arms and legs again, although they were throbbing with pain, and my head felt like I'd been on a Tilt-A-Whirl for the past three days. When I sat up, the world spun around me. It seemed that I should eat, but the mere thought of food made my stomach clench.

All the adults were still asleep. Catherine and Alexander were splayed next to each other on the floor, while Cyrus was sprawled over the table, snoring loud enough to put the walruses to shame.

Erica, Mike, and Zoe were no longer in the hut. They had obviously recovered sooner than I had. I figured I should try to find them.

I struggled to my feet and staggered out the door. Even though the air smelled like shellfish that had been through the digestive systems of a thousand walruses, it was still fresher than the snodgrass-tainted air in the Quonset hut—and so it made me feel better. Not a whole lot better, but still, it was something.

I looked up and down the shoreline for my friends. Instead, I saw the lumpy bodies of walruses, writhing under a slate-gray sky.

The walrus population had increased greatly overnight, so the great, blubbery beasts had colonized even more of the beach. They were piled up all around the Quonset hut, forcing me to pick my way through them. It was unsettling to be surrounded by so many enormous animals; even though walruses are herbivores and not very aggressive, if one had merely rolled over as I was walking past, it could have flattened me. Up close, walruses are extremely odd-looking, with bulging eyes and Lorax mustaches. Plus, they can change color.

More walruses were hauling themselves out of the ocean every minute, swimming ashore among the crashing waves— and unlike the ones that had been on the beach, which were brown, like I expected walruses to be—the new arrivals were all white. Not a bright white, but a kind of muted white that made them look like a bunch of walrus ghosts. This was a result of the walruses shunting blood around in their bodies. The blood vessels in their skin constrict in cold water to help them conserve heat, and so they turn pale. Even stranger, when walruses warm up, the blood returns to their skin and makes them bright pink. So in addition to the spooky white walruses, there were also plenty of walruses around that looked as though they had been dipped in Pepto-Bismol.

I didn't know any of the science behind this at the time. Instead, I thought I was hallucinating. I figured that seeing pink walruses was a bizarre side effect of snodgrass inhalation. It was disturbing, but then, I had plenty of other things to be worried about at the moment.

Like being marooned on Crooked Island, for starters. And Ivan Shumovsky's doomsday plan.

In the distance, across the sea, I could see the faint outline of the mainland. It was much too far to swim, and there didn't appear to be any boats on the island.

However, it would have only been a short helicopter flight. As far as I knew, Murray Hill hadn't been able to fly a helicopter when I'd last seen him, but if there had been a how-to manual among the books he'd been abandoned with, then it was possible he could have taught himself. Murray was the worst operator of moving vehicles that I had ever met, but there was little to run into between us and the mainland, so it was conceivable he could have made it. It would have been risky for an amateur, but then, given the choice between a lifetime on Crooked Island or a possibility of escape, I could understand why Murray had taken the chance.

Not far from the spot where the helicopter had been, I spotted Zoe. She was sitting on a bleached tree trunk, staring out at sea.

The trunk had obviously been brought there by the ocean. There were no trees anywhere near that size on Crooked Island. It was a two-ton piece of driftwood.

I lurched over to Zoe, which took far longer than it would have if I had been feeling good. My legs were barely functioning, and I had a labyrinth of flatulent pink walruses to negotiate. Still, Zoe didn't notice me coming until I was almost on top of her. When she turned to face me, she looked absolutely miserable.

I still asked her how she was feeling, just to be polite.

"Well, let's see," she replied. "I've been drugged and marooned on the bleakest, coldest, smelliest island on earth while some revenge-driven Russian is plotting doomsday for Alaska. So, I'd say this is pretty much the worst I've felt in my entire life. How are you?"

"About the same." I slumped onto the tree trunk next to her. "Any idea where Erica and Mike are?"

"They're off exploring the island, looking for anything we can use to rescue ourselves. I tried to join them, but . . . like I said, I'm not doing so good."

"Me neither." It made sense that Erica and Mike would have recovered from the sedation faster than we had. They were in the best shape of any of us. It seemed to me that I should probably go help them, but my body still felt like I'd fallen down a flight of stairs. So I figured I could take a little more time to recuperate; for all I knew, we were going to be stuck on Crooked Island for months.

Although my body was aching, my brain was starting to think better in the fresh air. A thought came to me. "Are you sure there isn't something else bothering you?"

"Besides the drugging and the marooning and doomsday? That isn't enough?"

"It's just that yesterday, back when we were on Kodiak Island, after we rescued Cyrus . . . you seemed out of sorts. Like something was wrong."

Zoe pulled her gaze from the ocean to look at me. "Was it that noticeable?"

"To *me* it was. I'm not sure about the others. What happened?"

Zoe returned to staring at the ocean. "You wouldn't understand."

"I might. Give me a chance."

Zoe still didn't say anything.

Down on the shore, a walrus let out what might have been the loudest expulsion of gas in recorded history. It sounded like a bomb going off.

I thought back to everything that had happened on Kodiak Island. My brain was still sluggish, but I managed to pinpoint the approximate time that Zoe had started acting strange. I remembered her gasping with astonishment when she had first entered the room to find Erica fighting with Svetlana—and after that, she hadn't been herself.

"Does this have something to do with Svetlana?"

Zoe turned back to me, alarmed, indicating I was right. But she remained silent.

"You seemed surprised when you first saw her," I recalled. "Did you recognize her? Did you learn about her in an evil villain seminar or something?"

"No. I'd never seen her until that moment."

"Did she frighten you?"

"Well . . . yeah. In a way."

"What do you mean?"

Zoe held my gaze for a long time, as if grappling with whether or not she should share what she was thinking with me. Finally, she said, "I think that Svetlana and I had a moment."

It took me a bit longer than it should have to realize what she meant. And even then, I wasn't sure I understood her correctly. My brain wasn't operating at full speed yet. "You mean . . . a romantic moment?"

"No, a nauseating moment," Zoe said sarcastically. "Of course a romantic moment!"

"What was it like?"

"Well . . . I guess it was kind of like when you saw Erica for the first time. How did that feel?"

I thought back to that encounter. Even though it had happened a year and a half earlier, I remembered it perfectly, because it was one of the most powerful events of my life. Erica had just tackled me in the midst of an incredibly stressful entrance exam at spy school where I thought I was under attack by enemy agents. And yet, the second I saw her, even with everything else going on, I was smitten. "Like getting hit by lightning."

"Exactly. I've never felt anything like this before."

"Not even with me?"

"No." Zoe shook her head. "Sorry. I mean, I liked you and all . . . but this was different."

I nodded understanding, my pride only slightly bruised, and then I thought of something. "You said that you *and* Svetlana had a moment. Not only you."

"Right. When I came into the room, our eyes met, and . . . I think we had a connection."

I tried to recall the circumstances, which wasn't easy, as a lot had been going on at the time. But I had a faint recollection of Svetlana dropping her guard when Zoe and Mike showed up.

"Are you sure Svetlana wasn't distracted by Mike?" I asked. "He's awfully handsome."

Zoe slugged me in the shoulder. Hard. "What am I, chopped liver?"

"No, but . . . well . . . are you *positive* she was looking at you?"

"I thought she was, but . . . there's no way to know for sure, right?" Zoe sighed and put her face in her hands. "Maybe she *was* looking at Mike."

I was still replaying the events of the previous day, trying to make sense of them myself. Svetlana had been on the edge of the bog when our helicopter took off, watching us through binoculars. Had she come to see Zoe again? Or Mike? It could have just as easily been either of them. Or had she come for an entirely different purpose altogether? After all, she was a spy for the Russians, and we were her enemies. She had a vested interest in knowing how we were escaping, the direction we were heading, and what type of helicopter we were flying. I hated to admit it, but of the many reasons Svetlana might have been watching us, a sudden mutual crush on Zoe seemed the least likely to me.

Not that I was going to tell Zoe that. She was miserable enough as it was.

"Ugh," she groaned. "Of all the people in the world to fall for like this, I can't believe I fell for *her*."

"Because she's a girl?"

Zoe leveled me with a stare that said I might be the biggest moron on the planet. "No. Because she's *evil*." She groaned again. "Her family is plotting some massive doomsday scheme—and the only thing I can think is, *Great. It'll give me a chance to see her again.* I couldn't fall for someone at the local pizza parlor or the car wash. No, I have to fall for my sworn enemy."

"It's not like you had a whole lot of other options," I said, hoping it sounded supportive. "You were just saying yesterday that you've had no chance to meet anyone new. Svetlana's the only person your age you've seen in the last month. Heck, you've barely seen any other humans at all."

"That's right," Erica agreed.

Zoe and I both yelped in fright, startled to realize she was right behind us.

"Could you please not sneak up on us like that?" I asked. "We're on edge enough as it is."

"I *didn't* sneak up on you," Erica protested. "In fact, I made plenty of noise. But I guess you didn't hear me over the wind and the walruses."

On the beach nearby, as if to emphasize how noisy they were, a walrus burped so loud that it sounded like a cannon blast.

"How much of our conversation did you hear?" Zoe asked.

"Most of it," Erica replied.

Zoe flushed, embarrassed. "That was supposed to be a secret."

"Just like what you said in the trainer yesterday," Erica reported. "About how lonely you've been feeling . . ."

"Wait," Zoe interrupted. "You heard that?"

"Of course."

"But the trainer was really loud and you had noise-cancelling headphones on. And you were busy trying not to crash."

"My hearing is *really* good," Erica said.

"You didn't even react when I yelled 'Erica stinks,'" I noted.

"Oh, right." Erica socked me in the arm. "There's my reaction. Satisfied?"

"Not really," I muttered.

Erica returned her attention to Zoe. "The point is, you admitted that you were very lonely. And now, suddenly, someone new and exciting shows up. It's only natural that you think that you've connected. . . ."

"I didn't *think* we connected," Zoe corrected. "I felt it."

"You were barely in the room with her," Erica said dismissively. "There was no time to connect."

Zoe stiffened, annoyed. "I'm not letting the Ice Queen lecture me on relationships. You didn't even know that you had a crush on Ben until I told you."

Erica nodded, conceding the point. "I'll admit that I've been somewhat emotionally stunted in the past. But I've been studying the psychology of interpersonal connections to try to understand it better. It turns out that where romance is concerned . . . most humans are a mess."

Zoe grew even more annoyed. "Are you saying that *I'm* a mess?"

"Well, you're human. So statistically, there's a good chance that's the case. Humans often have crushes on people they don't even know based on virtually nothing. They routinely fall in love with people who treat them poorly and then reject potential mates who would be perfect for them.

Even with *millions* of potential mates available, humans often struggle to find even one that they can have a decent, supportive relationship with. Honestly, it's a wonder that we've managed to survive as a species."

A walrus belched resoundingly.

"You'd rather be one of them?" Zoe asked, pointing to the mass of wrinkly pinnipeds.

Erica said, "Most animals assess the worth of a potential mate through a careful analysis of its health, strength, and virility. Emotion doesn't factor into it one bit. And it's worked out pretty well for them for the last few million years—until humans showed up."

I asked, "So you think emotions aren't important in forming relationships?"

"They complicate things and mess up our ability to think rationally. Plus, they can cause a whole lot of trouble. While there are certainly emotions that make you feel good, like happiness and excitement, there are a heck of a lot more that make us feel bad: sadness, anger, disgust, fear, loneliness, annoyance, jealousy, doubt, guilt, desperation, anxiety, frustration, worry, terror, shame, grief, paranoia, desperation, disappointment, nervousness—and, of course, love."

"Um . . . ," I said. "Love is a *good* emotion."

"Not always." Erica looked to Zoe. "How are you feeling right now?"

"Crummy," Zoe replied.

"See?" Erica said. "Not so good."

"I'm not in love with Svetlana," Zoe said defensively. "I don't even know her! I'd just like the chance to see her again."

"I wouldn't count on that happening any time soon," Erica said.

"I know." Zoe sighed miserably. "Maybe you're right. Life *would* be better without all these stupid emotions."

At that point, Mike came slouching along a thin trail that circled the island. He looked almost as downcast as Zoe.

"Why's everyone looking so glum?" he asked.

"Apparently, we have too many emotions," Zoe replied grumpily.

"Emotions?" Mike asked curiously. "No. What we have too much of here is walrus manure."

"What Zoe means is—" Erica began, but Zoe delivered a look so sharp that even Erica seemed scared by it. The message was clear: Zoe didn't want anyone else knowing about her crush on Svetlana.

Mike didn't notice. He was too busy moping. "I've circled this entire island. Remember how a couple months ago, we were stranded in the jungle in Mexico, and I was complaining about that being the worst thing ever?"

"Yes," Erica, Zoe, and I answered at once.

"Well, I was totally wrong." Mike sat down heavily on

the dead tree trunk. "The jungle was paradise compared to this place. It was hot. There was plenty of fresh water. There was food to eat. And we weren't too far from some very nice beach resorts. This place is freezing, it's a hundred miles from the nearest town, and there's nothing to eat."

"There's walrus," I suggested.

"Yeah, good luck with that," Mike grumped. "There's a dead walrus in the next cove over. And disgusting as that may be, it's still this island's number one tourist attraction. I figured I should see what it might take to eat one. First of all, their skin is impossible to cut through. It's like wrinkly concrete. I busted my hunting knife on it. Walruses are the coconuts of sea mammals. But then I found a little gash on the tail where it looked like maybe a shark had bitten it. The skin was gone, and there was some meat showing."

"What did it taste like?" Zoe asked.

"I don't know," Mike replied. "It smelled so bad, I figured I'd rather starve than eat it."

"That might change once we run out of food," Erica warned.

"Which is a very likely possibility." Mike ran his hands through his hair in despair. "We're on an island in the middle of nowhere, we have no phone service or radios or any other way to contact help, and we'd already gone off the grid, so it could be *weeks* before anyone even notices we're missing.

Maybe more. So yeah, I think we're all gonna be eating walrus burgers, because there's zero chance that we're getting rescued anytime soon."

"I'm not so sure about that," someone said.

We all spun around.

A young woman was standing on the hill behind us. And while it normally would have been astounding to see her there, apparently having materialized out of thin air on our remote island, there was something even more astonishing about her appearance:

I *knew* her.

WILDLIFE SMUGGLING

The *Beluga*
The Bering Sea
Somewhere southwest of Kwigillingok, Alaska
July 18
1200 hours

Tina Cuevo had been my resident advisor when I had first come to spy school. Resident advisors were older students tasked with overseeing younger students in the dormitory. At normal schools, they might help students deal with homework-related stress and disputes over use of the laundry machines. At spy school, they had significantly more dangerous duties; on my first night, Tina had to deal with an assassin who'd come to kill me.

Unfortunately, Murray Hill had taken advantage of Tina's kindness in his first plot for SPYDER, and Tina's reputation had been badly tarnished. She had still been allowed to graduate, but the CIA had punished her by sending her to Vancouver, Canada. While most people consider Vancouver to be one of the loveliest cities on earth, it is extremely safe and has virtually no international intrigue, which makes it unappealing for aspiring CIA agents. When I had last seen Tina, she had been very unhappy about her posting, believing that her career there would be filled with tedious investigations into uninspired crimes—if there were any crimes to investigate at all.

But things had turned out much better than she had expected.

"I'm on the International Wildlife Anti-Smuggling Task Force!" she informed me excitedly. "It's awesome!"

We were standing at the bow of the *Beluga*, the Coast Guard cutter that had brought her to Crooked Island, along with eight able-bodied coastguardsmen. After rousing Cyrus, Alexander, and Catherine from their snodgrass-induced slumber, we had all boarded the boat, which was now slicing through the arctic waters on its way to the Army National Guard base on Toksook Bay, a few hundred miles north.

The others were all gathered in the pilothouse, which was enclosed and heated, except for Alexander, who was so prone to seasickness, he couldn't even sleep on a waterbed. He was at the opposite end of the boat, clinging to the railing and occasionally vomiting over the stern. (The captain had advised him to stay at the back of the boat, rather than the front, because that way he wouldn't be puking into the wind, which was always a disaster.) Tina and I were catching up outside because I felt slightly nauseated myself—although I wasn't sure if this was due to the motion of the boat or the residual effects of being sedated—and it helped to have fresh air and look at the horizon.

The arctic wind was bracing, and cold ocean spray kept splattering us, but the Coast Guard had provided me—and everyone else—with warm clothes and waterproof jackets for the ride. They also had plenty of food. Inside, my friends were devouring warm oatmeal and hot cocoa, while Tina had given me a thermos of tea.

"I thought you *hated* the idea of combatting wildlife smugglers," I reminded her. "You said it'd be dull."

"I was wrong! It's amazing! On my very first day, we busted some jerks trying to smuggle a baby tiger into Canada. I saved its life—and it was adorable! Since then, I've saved hundreds of other animals: monkeys and parrots and pangolins and snakes and lizards and even a giant panda. So the Agency sent me up here, where I could work the front lines against the smugglers and poachers . . . as well as dealing with some other threats to our country."

"Like what?"

"For starters, this is as close to Russia as you can get in the US. In the lower forty-eight states, everyone considers the Cold War a thing of the past, but I can assure you, it's alive and well up here."

"I've noticed," I said, thinking of Ivan.

"And then I had to keep an eye on our old friend Murray."

I turned to her, surprised. "That was your job?"

"Well, they couldn't just leave him alone on an island for the rest of his life. Someone had to drop by every now and then to deliver his canned food and make sure he hadn't escaped. So I volunteered."

"Why? After what Murray did to you, I figured you'd despise him."

"I *do*. Which was why it was always a treat to see how much he was suffering. He was so wonderfully miserable there . . . until all of you let him escape." For the first time since we'd reunited, Tina frowned.

"Sorry about that. He tricked us."

"Join the club."

At the stern of the boat, Alexander vomited boisterously once again.

The *Beluga* plowed into a wave, kicking up a sheen of

water that splattered us. I wiped my face dry, then asked, "So it was just luck that you happened to be making your visit to the island this morning?"

"No. The emergency alert system triggered, indicating that something was wrong."

"How does that work?"

"There actually is Wi-Fi on the island, in case of emergencies, although it has a very weak signal. I let Murray know about it but then refused to give him the password. So of course, he was always trying to guess what it was."

"How often?"

"About every five minutes. It was pretty much the only thing he did. However, the system was designed to record every access attempt. . . ."

"So when he stopped trying, you knew something was wrong."

"Exactly. Although I didn't think he'd escaped. I thought there was a much better chance that he'd gotten sick from eating rancid kelp—or been mauled by a walrus." Tina grinned, as though the thought pleased her. "But I had to be cautious, just in case he'd truly managed something devious, like aligning himself with the Russians. That's why we didn't approach the island from the direction where you could see us coming. We docked on the other side, then came over the top. I thought of a lot of possibilities as to what I might find, but you were pretty much the *last* person I expected to see."

"I wasn't expecting to see you, either," I replied.

"What happened?"

"Murray sedated us with some local herb he'd learned about and then stole our helicopter."

Understanding suddenly dawned on Tina. "Was it an old Russian model?"

"Yes. A Yukutsk 260."

"Oh. Everything makes sense now. An old Russian copter was found wrecked in the forest near Manokotak this morning."

"And you didn't connect that to Murray's sudden disappearance?"

Tina bristled slightly at my accusation. "First of all, no one had any idea *when* the copter crashed. It could have been weeks ago. And when most people discover a Russian helicopter on American soil, their general concern is that it belonged to the *Russians*. Especially up in these parts. How was I to know that all of you were going to screw up and hand deliver a helicopter to Murray? I didn't even know he could fly."

"I don't think he can. How far away from Crooked Island is Mammackattack?"

"Manokotak. Maybe twenty miles."

"He's lucky he got that far. Is there a town near there?"

"Not a very big one."

"Well, he's probably headed that way. Murray's not one for wilderness survival."

"No. With any luck, he'll starve to death. Or get eaten by a wolverine."

"Still, we ought to put out an alert."

Tina got on her satellite phone and did just that. It was designed to work in remote areas, but the reception was still spotty. It took Tina a while to get in touch with her superiors and bring them up to speed on what had happened.

I watched the western coast of Alaska slide by while she handled things. Untamed wilderness stretched as far as I could see.

After Tina hung up, she asked, "What were all of you even doing with a Yukutsk 260 anyhow?"

"A really rich computer programmer gave it to Alexander as a gift in return for us saving him from Joshua Hallal in England."

Tina now looked less offended and more jealous. "You got to go on a mission to England?"

"Er . . . yes."

"Why?"

"To defeat SPYDER."

Tina's jaw dropped in astonishment. "*You* defeated the most dangerous evil secret organization in modern times?"

"Yes. With the help of everyone else here. You didn't know that?"

"I heard rumors that SPYDER had been defeated. But as for how . . . well, that's classified of course. I can't believe it was *you*. I mean, no offense, but a year and a half ago, you didn't have the slightest idea what to do if you found a single assassin in your room."

"It was my first night at spy school! And I defeated him."

"You got lucky."

"Maybe. But I won."

"Still, I can't believe you're facing off against SPYDER in England while I'm stuck out here in the boonies."

"I thought you said you liked it out here."

"I *do*! It's just not exactly glamorous. Next thing I know, you're going to tell me you've also been to Paris."

I pursed my lips, which was all it took to set Tina off.

"Oh for Pete's sake. Paris too? Where else?"

"Mexico. Panama. Vail."

Tina laughed despite herself. "Unbelievable. And yet, you always were a smart cookie, Ripley. You caught Murray the first time when no one else at the CIA had any idea what was going on. So I guess maybe you earned all this."

"Maybe," I repeated. "Although I've ended up on a lot of these missions due to bad luck. This one just kind of fell into our laps."

"Speaking of which, how *did* you end up on Crooked Island?"

I told Tina the whole story. She did her best not to interrupt too much, although she couldn't keep herself from telling me how lucky I was when she heard that I'd been attacked by a submarine and infiltrated a Russian compound.

When I got to the end of it all, she fell silent for a while, staring out at the sea ahead of us. Finally, she said, "I was wondering if something like this might happen."

"Why? Have you heard of Shumovsky before?"

"No. But I've heard plenty of chatter about old Russian agents unhappy about the American purchase of Alaska. It seems a lot of the folks posted in Siberia think it was a mistake for Russia to offer Alaska up for sale in the first place."

"That happened a long time ago."

"Some people really hold a grudge. Do you know why Russia wanted to get rid of Alaska in the first place?"

"Because it's only forty degrees in the middle of July?"

"Nope. Sea otters."

"Sea otters?" I repeated, not sure if I had heard correctly.

"Yup. The wildlife trade is much more important in world affairs than you might realize. Back in the 1800s, it pretty much drove international politics. All those explorers who headed across North America, staking claims for various countries . . . they were looking for furs. That's where the big money was. And no animal's fur was worth more than that of the sea otter."

"Why?"

In the distance, a pod of whales surfaced, blasting jets of mist from their blowholes.

Tina pointed to them. "Those whales, and practically every other mammal that lives in these waters, have blubber to keep warm. But sea otters don't. Instead, they have the densest fur of any animal in the world: a million hairs per square inch, while you probably don't have one hundred thousand on your entire head."

"I think Cyrus might have that much in his ears."

Tina gave me a smirk, then continued. "Sea otter pelts are amazingly soft and warm. And Russia is a *really* cold country. For the Russians, sea otter pelts were one of the greatest discoveries of all time. They were worth fifty bucks a piece in the late 1800s, which is like several thousand dollars now. That's what drove Russia's exploration of Alaska and their claims to the territory. They also killed seals and foxes for their pelts, and they fished, too, but otters were the main attraction. They went after them big time. So guess what happened?"

"They wiped the otters out."

"Bingo. Nearly drove them to extinction. Just like we've done with almost every other animal species. Without sea otters, Alaska didn't seem so worthwhile anymore. It took a lot of resources to supply the territory, and Russia was in serious debt after the Crimean War. They figured the time was right to sell Alaska to the United States. The purchase was very popular in America, and it was negotiated surprisingly fast. The US got a bargain. The seven point two million dollars they spent is equal to just over a hundred and forty million dollars today. There are homes in Malibu that cost more than that! And for that money, the US got well over half a million square miles of land that was incredibly rich in resources. Within only a year of the purchase, prospectors found a vein of gold that easily paid for the entire cost of Alaska. And that paled in comparison to the Klondike Gold Rush thirty years later. Or the discovery of oil in the 1970s."

"So all these Russian guys think Russia really got the bad end of that deal."

"Exactly. From any perspective, the decision to sell was shortsighted, at best. If Russia had held on to Alaska, the country would certainly be a heck of a lot richer now, not to mention having strategic control of almost the entire Arctic. And if what Murray told you was actually true about the Croatoan robbing them blind, then they didn't get *anything* in return for giving up the territory. Which is going to be even *more* upsetting to these hard-liners."

"I guess so," I agreed.

The *Beluga* plunged into a deep trough between waves, forcing us to duck as a spray of frigid water sailed over the bow.

Tina said, "Of course, there's one other thing that tends to get forgotten in all of this grappling over Alaska."

"What's that?"

"There were people here long before Russia and the United States ever even knew this place existed. Russia took this land from them—and treated them terribly, by the way—and when the United States bought it, the Alaska Natives weren't consulted or paid one cent."

"Do you think maybe they could have been involved in Operation Hornswoggle? To get even with the Russians?"

"No. But honestly, if they found some way to rebel against either country, I wouldn't blame them. In truth, the US has probably given the Alaska Natives a slightly better deal than any indigenous tribe in the lower forty-eight states, but that was an awfully low bar to clear. A few of the original tribes were able to hold on to some of their ancestral lands up here, although we still took plenty."

I nodded agreement. Our temporary spy school in Kenai Fjords had been built on land that was once important to the native people. But then, so was our original spy school in Washington, DC—as was everything else in North America.

A pod of our boat's namesake animals suddenly appeared

in the sea alongside us. The beluga whales were beautiful and graceful, with sleek white skin—and they made a surprising array of sounds: sneezelike blasts of air from their blowholes, shrill whistles, and deep, sonorous rumbles. Despite the gravity of what Tina and I had just been discussing, I was delighted to see them and called to the others to join us.

Everyone rushed outside and crowded along the rail to watch as the whales skimmed through the water around us. Erica was downright giddy at the sight of them, reminding me that, despite her incredible skills and unusual maturity, she was still a teenage girl at heart. Even Cyrus appeared unusually joyful upon seeing them. The only exception was Alexander, who moaned in agony from the stern. "How much longer until we reach our destination?"

"I'm afraid it's still another few hours," the captain reported, provoking a whimper of dismay from Alexander.

"You should be happy," Cyrus informed his son. "We might've been on this boat a whole lot longer heading to our next rendezvous with Ivan. But while you've been lollygagging out here, the rest of us have been hard at work, using the radios and putting a plan together."

"I'm not lollygagging," Alexander replied defensively. "I'm just gagging, period. I'm seasick." He turned to face us, revealing that his skin had turned the greenish color of canned peas.

"We're meeting Ivan again?" I asked.

"He told us to find out about Operation Hornswoggle," Cyrus replied. "And we're gonna give him the news. I managed to get word to him that we have the info he wants, and we found a neutral meeting space where neither side can ambush the other."

"We *thought* we would have to take this boat all the way there," Catherine added, "but it turns out that the National Guard base in Toksook Bay has a helicopter they can lend us."

"How'd you swing that?" Alexander asked.

"You know how charming I can be." Catherine flashed a winning smile. "And also, we pulled rank. Your father has a lot of clout in these parts. Of course, I had to be a bit cagey when discussing what had happened to our last helicopter. I'm sure the National Guard would prefer that theirs not get stolen."

"What would all of us and Ivan consider a neutral space?" I asked. "Where are we going?"

"No-man's-land," said Catherine.

NEUTRAL TERRITORY

No-Man's-Land

The Chukchi Sea

One hundred miles west of Point Hope, Alaska

July 18

1900 hours

No-man's-land was an inaccurate name for where we were headed. Because there wasn't any land there at all.

Ivan didn't want to meet on United States territory, and there was no way that Cyrus would risk meeting on Russian territory. So they had to find someplace in the middle.

All the islands in the Bering Strait between Russia and the United States had been claimed by one of those countries. But north of the Arctic Circle, there was ice.

There was far less ice now, in the heart of summer, than there would have been in winter. (And, as Catherine had pointed out, thanks to climate change, there was far less ice now than there used to be.) However, there was still enough for our purposes. Out the window of our borrowed helicopter, I could see hundreds of ice floes floating on the surface of the sea. These hadn't calved off a glacier, like the ones in the fjord near our camp; instead, they were remnants of the ice sheet that had covered most of the Arctic Ocean the previous winter. And so, many of them were extremely large; some were several miles across.

Ivan had selected one that was about the size of a football field. It was relatively round, although the edges were jagged. Ivan and his fellow Russians had arrived before us, then sent the coordinates. As we homed in, I could see their own helicopter parked at one end of the floe, while the Russians waited for us in the middle.

The Toksook National Guard base had lent us a Sea Knight helicopter, which was slightly larger than the old Russian one that Murray had stolen from us. It was also louder, as there was a set of rotors at both ends, so all of us had noise-cancelling headphones clamped over our ears. As with our old chopper, the interior was designed for function rather than comfort. There were jump seats along the walls and a good amount of empty space inside.

The army had outfitted us with other things as well: They'd fed us a hot meal, then given us additional rations, all-weather gear to make up for what we'd lost when the trainer exploded, and some weapons—although they had been very insistent that those were for the adults to use and not the teenagers. In fact, they had been intrigued as to why a bunch of teenagers was going on a mission at all, but Cyrus had silenced their questions by flashing his CIA badge and telling them the operation was classified.

Before we landed, Alexander made a pass over the ice floe to survey the enemy. We came in close enough that we could make out the individuals who were gathered below. There were five Russians. Ivan was there, along with three agents who I recognized from Fort King: big, burly men who now sported fresh bruises, thanks to Erica. Ivan smiled and waved to us as we hovered overhead, as though we were friends joining him for a picnic.

The fifth member of the team was Svetlana. While the men wore bulky parkas, Svetlana sported a surprisingly fashionable winter camouflage ensemble, with a hooded anorak and matching muck boots. She looked as though she had just come from a photo shoot for *Arctic Warfare Weekly*. Between the mottled white of her clothing and her white-blond hair, she blended into the ice almost as well as a polar bear would have.

Beside me, Zoe's eyes lit up in excitement upon seeing her. Then she realized I had noticed this and grew embarrassed. She leaned close to me so that I could hear her over the whirr of the rotors—or at least read her lips. "I know I'm not supposed to have a crush on the enemy, but I can't help it."

"It's okay," I assured her, even though I was pretty sure that it wasn't.

"Do you think she came to see me?"

I considered lying again and telling Zoe there was a chance this was true, but I couldn't see any point to it. I didn't want to give Zoe false hope—and we needed her to be focused on the mission instead of Svetlana. "I'm guessing Ivan gave her orders to show up."

Zoe's excitement drained, and her eyes drooped, making me feel terrible for what I'd said. "Yeah. I guess that makes sense," she agreed dourly.

I tried to come up with something to say that might lift her spirits—while not creating unreal expectations. Nothing came to mind. Instead, all I could think of was to try to distract her. I pointed out the window at an ice floe in the distance and said, "Oooh! Is that a polar bear?"

"Stop trying to distract me," Zoe said.

"I wasn't trying to do that," I lied. "I really think there's a polar bear over there."

"Great," Zoe muttered. "Now, in addition to rejection and Russian sneak attacks, I also have to worry about getting eaten."

"Oh." As it turned out, there actually *was* a polar bear on a neighboring ice floe. It was a good distance from ours, but now I was worried about getting eaten as well.

I pressed my face against the window, trying to get a better look at the bear, just as Alexander banked suddenly. My forehead jounced off the glass, and I nearly fell out of my jump seat.

On the other side of the helicopter, Mike snickered at me.

Cyrus must have felt that the Russians looked trustworthy enough, because Alexander was bringing the helicopter in for a landing. Outside the window, the twin rotors kicked up a blizzard as we lowered onto the opposite side of the floe that the Russians had parked on. Alexander touched down perfectly and shut the helicopter off.

As the blades stopped whirring, the sound quickly dropped from deafening to incredibly quiet.

The Sea Knight was designed to haul vehicles, if needed, with a drop-down ramp at the rear. Alexander flipped a switch and it lowered, allowing arctic air to gust into the helicopter.

Even though we'd been outfitted with weapons, they

were only for emergencies. Cyrus and Ivan had agreed that no one would bring them to our meeting, so we left them in the helicopter, which made me uneasy. I didn't like carrying a weapon myself—but I also didn't like the idea of all of us going to face the Russians unarmed. It felt like we were walking into a lion's den.

Alexander had agreed to stay behind with the helicopter, in case of trouble. He was chosen because he was the only one who knew how to fly the chopper—and because Cyrus felt that the farther Alexander was from the meeting, the less chance he had of screwing things up.

"Here goes nothing," Cyrus said, and then led us down the ramp.

As I stepped out onto the ice floe, it occurred to me that I had never been so far from land in my life. Even though I had been on a mission aboard a cruise ship rather recently, we had never been more than a few miles off the coast. The ice I was standing on was a dozen times farther out. All the color in the world appeared to have vanished except for shades of blue (the sky and the sea) and white (the ice and the distant polar bear). There wasn't a plant, or a rock, or even a bit of dirt to be seen. We were floating in the middle of nowhere.

Still, it was as nice a day as we could have hoped for in the Arctic. The sun was shining and reflecting off the white floe so strongly that I felt its warmth despite standing atop a giant ice cube. It was deathly quiet, save for the faint slap of the water against the floes and the distant huffing of the polar bear. Despite the brisk wind, the sea was as calm and level as the Great Plains. The floe was so big and sturdy, it felt as though we were walking across solid ground.

It wasn't flat, though. Instead, the surface varied every few feet, as though trying to display how many different ways ice could form. In some places, the ice was in jumbled slabs like a sidewalk ruptured by an earthquake; in other places, brittle spikes jutted upward, so it looked like a field of frozen porcupines; and in yet other places, it was full of holes, like an enormous hunk of Swiss cheese, or as lumpy as bad oatmeal, or as slick and slippery as, well . . . an ice rink. Traversing it all was tricky, but we slowly made our way to the center.

As we walked, the cold of the ice began to overpower the heat of the sun. I could feel it rising through my body from my feet, chilling me.

The Russians kept their eyes locked on us the entire time, watching us carefully as we approached, like they were expecting trouble at any moment. We kept our eyes locked on them, too—except for the times when we had to look down to negotiate the various frozen obstacles, which was quite often. I was also on the lookout for trouble, and so was everyone else on my team, with the exception of Zoe, who was mooning over Svetlana.

Svetlana was not mooning over Zoe. Instead, she stared at all of us with a gaze that was even colder than the ice we were crossing.

Finally, we arrived at the center of the floe. Cyrus stopped ten yards away from the Russians, and we all followed his lead. At this distance, we were too far for them to suddenly sneak attack us, but close enough to be easily heard in the near silence of our surroundings.

The Russians unbuttoned their heavy jackets, showing us—to my great relief—that there were no weapons hidden underneath them.

We did the same thing, indicating that we intended for this to be a peaceful event.

Then we quickly buttoned up again, because it was cold.

In other businesses, meetings started with small talk. Like, *It's good to see you again* or *Did you have any trouble finding the location?*

Ivan dispensed with all that. "This meeting is happening much earlier than I expected," he said, his voice laden with suspicion.

"You made it clear you wanted the info ASAP," Cyrus replied. "We found a way to get it without having to schlep all the way to Washington. I thought you'd be happy about that."

"I *am* happy," Ivan replied.

"He doesn't *look* happy," Mike whispered to me, echoing

my own thoughts. "He looks like someone who just sat on a thumbtack."

"Let's hear this information, then," Ivan demanded. "What did you learn about Operation Hornswoggle?"

"It's not what you were expecting," Cyrus warned.

Ivan sneered at him. "I didn't ask for commentary. I asked for facts."

"All right," Cyrus said. "Don't say I didn't warn you. Here's the skinny: Hornswoggle wasn't hatched by the US government. We had nothing to do with it. It was a plot of the Croatoan, which is a covert group that has been scheming against America for over two hundred years. The United States' offer to purchase Alaska was completely legitimate. We paid you the seven point two million dollars fair and square. Your own ancestor witnessed the whole thing. And then the Croatoan robbed him blind."

Ivan's expression suddenly grew even more sour, as though he had now sat upon an entire box of thumbtacks. "You're saying my great-great-grandfather, Sergei Shumovsky, was taken advantage of?"

"I warned you that you wouldn't like this," Cyrus reminded him. "The US didn't screw the Russians out of Alaska. The Croatoan simply stole the payment."

"If Sergei was robbed, why didn't he report it?" Ivan asked.

"That's a question for Sergei, not me." Cyrus grinned,

enjoying Ivan's pained reaction. "I'm guessing that he was embarrassed and claimed the US was behind Hornswoggle to deflect the blame. But it's also possible that the Croatoan played him for a sap and really had him convinced that the US was behind this."

There was now a bit of color other than blue or white on the ice floe. Ivan had turned bright red in anger. "Are you claiming that my ancestor was either a liar or a fool?"

"Yes," Cyrus agreed. "And also, he wasn't very good at his job."

Ivan flushed even redder. He now looked like the inside of a raw steak.

Svetlana's expression had also changed. She no longer appeared cold and unemotional. But she wasn't angry like her grandfather. Instead, she seemed to be growing worried.

Ivan glared at Cyrus and spoke through gritted teeth. "Where did you get this information?"

"It came from a source who had worked inside the Croatoan," Cyrus replied. "He was imprisoned on Crooked Island in Alaska for his crimes. We visited him in person yesterday."

"And where is this source now?"

Cyrus's cocky grin faltered slightly. "He . . . er . . . gave us the slip."

"Your source got away? And you accuse *my* ancestor of being a bad spy?"

"I could have tracked him down again," Cyrus replied. "But that would have taken time . . . and I didn't have much of that, since you were threatening to set off this doomsday device. I thought it was more important to bring you the information you wanted, so that's what I did."

"It doesn't seem to me that you have any information at all," Ivan sneered. "You only have a half-baked story that insults my family."

"I recognize that this story may be insulting," Cyrus admitted. "But I assure you that it is fully baked."

"Then where is your proof?"

"If you'd like to give me more time to track down and recover our source, I'd be happy to do that."

"Here is what I think of your source." Ivan spat on the ice. "The word of a criminal is not proof of anything! I want documentation of your accusation!"

Now it was Cyrus who was beginning to look unsettled. "That doesn't exist anymore. The Croatoan destroyed all their files a few months ago."

"Let me see if I have this right," Ivan snarled. "I told you that I wanted the truth about Operation Hornswoggle. And instead, you come to me with an offensive tale told to you by an outlaw that you have no way to confirm. A tale that claims the great Sergei Shumovsky was a fool. And you expected me to be pleased with this?"

"No," Cyrus answered. "I didn't expect you to be pleased at all. But I did exactly as you requested. I brought you the information you wanted—at great risk to my own life, and the lives of my team. I met my end of the bargain. Now meet yours. Call off your doomsday plot."

"I will do no such thing," Ivan said. "America must suffer for her crimes against Russia."

The menace in his voice made my blood go cold. Or colder, given that I was already freezing. I glanced at the others on my team and saw they were all concerned as well. Even Erica.

Meanwhile, Cyrus looked offended, as though his reputation had just been questioned. "We had a deal."

"Which you failed to honor," Ivan growled.

"I did what you asked! If you don't accept that, then *you're* the one without honor!"

Ivan glared at Cyrus hatefully. "I am not going to let you insult my family and then slink back to Russia with my tail between my legs! You may think my ancestor was a fool, but I will prove to you that *I* am not one! You will pay for your offense—in blood!"

Ivan suddenly withdrew a device from his pocket. It was small enough to be mostly concealed by his hand, but it looked like a radio transmitter of some sort.

We were all too far away from Ivan to stop him from whatever he intended to do.

But Svetlana wasn't.

She suddenly sprang at her grandfather, bulldozing him off his feet and knocking the device from his grasp. Both Ivan and the device fell onto the ice.

"Svetlana!" Ivan cried. "Nyet!" He scrambled across the uneven surface of the floe on his belly, trying to recover the device, but Svetlana booted it away from him. It skittered across the ice and plunked into the sea in the distance.

Ivan wheeled on her. He appeared to be stunned, saddened, and livid all at once.

Then he turned to the three agents who had come with him and yelled something in Russian.

My Russian wasn't great, but I had learned a decent amount in spy school. Ivan had either yelled "detonate the charges" or "this duck smells like cheese."

Given the level of anger in his voice, I figured it was the former.

Although this was confirmed when Svetlana turned to all of us and shouted, "Run!"

DETONATION

No-Man's-Land

The Chukchi Sea

One hundred miles west of Point Hope, Alaska

July 18

1930 hours

Everyone on my team had expected that things might take a turn for the worse. Cyrus, Catherine, Erica, and Zoe immediately went into defensive positions, prepared for a fight.

"No!" Svetlana yelled at them, "You need to get off the ice. *Now!*"

And then she bolted away from the Russians, heading toward us.

This behavior all signaled that Svetlana knew something we didn't, so we listened to her.

We ran.

Catherine yelled desperately to Alexander, who was standing at the end of the rear ramp of the helicopter, watching us from a distance. "Start the chopper!"

Svetlana had more ground to cover than we did, but she was in exceptional shape and quickly narrowed the gap between us.

Although none of us could really move as fast as we wanted over the ice floe.

Imagine trying to run across something as slick and slippery as an ice rink. Then imagine trying to run across an ice rink that is full of frozen obstacles, like stumbling blocks and holes and porcupine-like balls of spikes. And then imagine that the entire surface was shaking violently.

The shaking began shortly after we started running for our lives, catching us all by surprise.

"What's going on?" Mike asked worriedly. "Is this an earthquake?"

"There's no earth to be quaking!" I yelled back.

"Maybe it's a tsunami, then?" Zoe suggested.

"That can't be it," Erica said. "The sea is still calm!" She pointed toward the water, which was, in fact, as still as glass.

"Then what's shaking us?" Mike asked.

A loud rumbling came from behind us. Even though we should have been focused on what lay ahead, we all turned around and looked back.

The conning tower of the Russian submarine erupted through the center of the floe, sending giant cubes of ice flying through the air.

"Oh," Mike said. "That answers my question."

Now, in addition to negotiating the obstacles on the floe, we also had to dodge the chunks of ice that were falling from the sky. Some were as big as canned hams.

And if all that wasn't bad enough, the ice floe had been structurally weakened by the sub puncturing through it. Large cracks swiftly spread out from the center, fracturing the icescape we were running across.

"Those sneaky Russians!" Catherine exclaimed. "They didn't just bring a chopper! They had an ambush planned all along!"

While this was extremely bad, I figured there was yet more in store for us. We still hadn't seen what Ivan had intended to use the detonator for.

A fissure was snaking its way through the ice behind us, cleaving the floe apart. Svetlana couldn't outrun it. The ice beneath her feet suddenly split open, and she dropped into the crevice with a startled yelp.

"Svetlana!" Zoe cried. She immediately spun around and ran back to the young Russian's aid.

"Don't help her!" Cyrus yelled. "She's the enemy!"

"She saved our lives!" Zoe yelled back. "Now I'm saving hers!"

Every one of my survival instincts was screaming at me, telling me it was suicide to turn back, but I did anyhow. I couldn't leave Zoe behind.

Mike turned back too. So did Catherine.

Erica turned as well, although she seemed extremely annoyed at herself for doing it. "This is a *terrible* idea," she muttered.

Svetlana had caught the edge of the fissure in the ice and was hanging from it by her fingertips. As we got closer, I could see down into the crevice. The sides plunged steeply through the floe into arctic water that would certainly chill Svetlana to death within seconds if she fell.

Svetlana was struggling to hold on to the ice, but her fingers were slipping.

Zoe was the first one to reach her, a few feet ahead of the rest of us. She arrived just as Svetlana lost her grip.

The Russian teen cried out in terror.

Zoe dove, skidded across the ice on her belly, and caught Svetlana's wrist at the last second.

Unfortunately, Zoe's momentum, combined with the

sudden added weight of Svetlana, now carried her toward the rim of the fissure too.

Mike and I both dove as well, each grabbing one of Zoe's ankles.

This prevented Zoe from being immediately dragged into the sea along with Svetlana, but we didn't completely stop her movement. And now her weight, along with Svetlana's, pulled both Mike and me along. Zoe slid into the fissure, while Mike and I ended up hanging partially over the edge, clinging to her ankles; Svetlana dangled below her, just above the surface of the sea.

In another few seconds, Mike and I were going to be dragged into the fissure ourselves. He and I did our best to fight this, but the ice was slippery, and there was nothing to hang on to.

For a brief moment, I thought about letting go.

This would have merely been following Chanda's First Maxim of Survival: It's impossible to save someone if you're dead yourself. If we let Zoe and Svetlana plunge into the water, then we had a shot at rescuing them, whereas if all four of us fell in, the odds weren't that good. It made perfect sense—and yet, I still felt like a heel for thinking it.

Plus, I knew Mike would never let go. He was too loyal to his friends. So I stubbornly held on too and hoped for the best.

There was a metallic twang behind me, and then something cinched tightly around my right ankle.

I stopped sliding across the ice with a sudden jolt. My ankle throbbed with pain, and my arms felt like they were going to be wrenched from their sockets—but I imagined that was still preferable to the sensation of freezing to death in the ocean.

"Hang on tight," Catherine said in an incredibly calm voice, given the circumstances. "We've got you."

I craned my neck to look behind me. Erica had jammed a grappling hook into the ice, then looped the wire around my ankle. She now knelt by my side, while Catherine knelt by Mike. They grabbed on to our parkas and heaved, dragging us away from the fissure.

Zoe's bottom half came with us, leaving her front end still hanging over the edge.

The Hales then grabbed on to Zoe and pulled her to safety, along with Svetlana.

I was winded, and my limbs felt like they'd been stretched like taffy. I took a second to catch my breath and gather my strength.

Which was a second too long for Cyrus. "Stop lazing around!" he yelled. "We've got to move!"

Sadly, he was right. The ice was continuing to come apart around us. Only a few feet away, a large chunk on the edge of the fissure calved off and plunged into the water.

Meanwhile, in the distance, the Russians were climbing into the submarine through a hatch in the hull. Ivan was the last one in. He paused halfway through, like a gopher poking out of its burrow, then looked across the ice toward us.

"Svetlana, come back!" he pleaded in Russian.

Svetlana glanced at him, as though considering this, then turned away. "We must go," she told us in English. Then she grabbed Zoe's hand, and they sprinted across the ice.

Even from a long distance, I could see Ivan flush red once again. The next time he spoke, it was in rage. "Obfuscate the jitterbug!" he howled.

Although, it's quite likely that my Russian wasn't good enough to translate him properly.

Erica freed my ankle from the grappling hook wire and helped me to my feet.

We dashed across the ice floe as fast as we could, along with everyone else on our team.

"Thanks for saving me back there," I told her. "Good thing you had a grappling hook with you."

"I *always* have a grappling hook with me," Erica said. "In case of emergencies like this."

"Really? Where do you keep it?"

"In my utility belt, of course." Even as we ran, Erica was folding the grappling hook and retracting the wire. Then she slipped it back into one of the pouches on her belt.

Ahead of us, Alexander had not started the helicopter yet. In fact, he wasn't even in the cockpit. Instead, he was frantically searching through his pockets.

"Why haven't you started the helicopter?" Catherine yelled at him.

"I can't remember where I put the keys!" Alexander yelled back.

"What?" Cyrus screamed in rage.

"I think I put them in a pocket!" Alexander explained. "But there's like a hundred pockets in this outfit, and I can't remember which was the right one!"

That made sense. Each article of our cold-weather gear had a dozen pockets: the jackets, the pants, and the lower layers as well. Even though I was annoyed at Alexander for misplacing his keys, I could easily understand how he'd done it.

Behind us, Ivan had disappeared into the submarine. Now a Russian agent popped out of the hatch. He had a gun clutched in his hand and started firing at the ice.

Mike laughed. "That guy can't even shoot straight! He's not aiming anywhere near us!"

"He's not trying to hit us," Svetlana said gravely. "He's trying to hit the explosive charges."

"Oh," I said, suddenly understanding. "*That's* what Ivan's detonator was for."

The Russian agent managed to strike his target. At the exact spot where we had been standing when we confronted Ivan, a ball of flame erupted from the ice, blasting a giant crater. The entire floe trembled even more violently than before, while significantly larger chunks of ice flew into the air. These were the size of basketballs.

"Those sneaky jerks booby-trapped the floe before we got here!" Cyrus exclaimed.

"And if it hadn't been for Svetlana, we would have been blown to smithereens," Mike added, looking to the Russian teen thankfully.

Svetlana looked uneasy about the praise. "There's more!" she warned.

Sure enough, the Russians hadn't set only one charge. A second triggered behind us, blasting yet another crater in the ice.

The floe trembled again. More cracks shot through it. It was starting to come apart beneath our feet.

At the same time, ice chunks were crashing down all around us like massive hailstones.

It was almost impossible to run across the shaking, collapsing floe, but we did our best. Fueled by fear and adrenaline, we skimmed through the obstacles and dodged the ice falling from the sky.

Ahead of us, Alexander was still frantically searching his pockets, unable to find the keys.

"Check your left front pants pocket!" Catherine called to Alexander.

Alexander did this, then grinned in relief. "Found them!" He happily jangled the keys in the air for us to see.

"Don't show them to us!" Catherine shouted. "*Use* them!"

"Right! Good idea, honey!" Alexander raced up the ramp toward the cockpit.

A third explosion triggered behind us, rocking the entire floe wildly. A section the size of a two-car garage snapped off just to my right, immediately creating a chasm in the ice.

In the cockpit, Alexander started the helicopter's engines.

The rotary blades began to turn, although slowly at first. It was going to take a little time for them to build up the speed to lift the helicopter off the ice.

And time was something we didn't have much of.

A fourth explosion triggered, even closer than the others. The entire floe broke apart, fracturing into five large pieces, like a jigsaw puzzle being disassembled. Thankfully, my friends and I all ended up on the same piece as our helicopter, although it was no longer nearly as stable as the large floe had been. Plus, the explosions were churning the water. Our section of the floe seesawed wildly on the waves.

Zoe, Cyrus, and I were all tossed off our feet. I landed hard on a smooth section that was like a natural Slip 'N Slide and would have shot right off the edge into the ocean if Erica hadn't grabbed my collar.

I scrambled back to my feet, and we started running again.

The blades were spinning faster now, but still not quite fast enough. As we closed in on it, the helicopter stubbornly refused to get airborne.

Then the section of the floe the copter was sitting on snapped off and sank.

The ice dropped away.

The helicopter almost sank with it.

But it didn't.

At the last possible moment, the blades began whirring fast enough to keep the helicopter in the air. Instead of plunging into the sea, it hovered just above the surface.

The rest of our ice floe was crumbling. More and more pieces were breaking off every second.

Alexander shifted the helicopter slightly closer to us so that it levitated just above the disintegrating ice, then swiveled it around so that the rear ramp was facing us.

A fifth explosion went off, so close that the concussion of air lifted me off my feet and carried me toward the helicopter. The floe shattered. Tons of ice went careening through the air. Most of it plunked into the ocean, but some landed on the rear blades of the Sea Knight, which instantly pureed it into slush and spit it back at us. It was as though we had been dropped into a gigantic snow cone machine.

We reached the helicopter as the floe came apart beneath our feet, splintering into a million pieces. If I had been a second later, I might have fallen into the sea, but I got to the ramp just in time. So did everyone else . . . almost.

Cyrus faltered at the last second. I wasn't sure why. He might have slipped or stumbled. Whatever the case, he was standing still when the ice gave way. He nearly dropped through the disintegrating floe, but Mike shifted his direction at the last moment and slammed into Cyrus from behind, knocking him forward onto the ramp.

Then the ice collapsed from under Mike, and he dropped beneath the ramp and vanished from sight.

15

RESCUE

No-Man's-Land

The Chukchi Sea

One hundred miles west of Point Hope, Alaska

July 18

1945 hours

I stood on the ramp, gaping in horror at the place where Mike had disappeared.

It was only for a few seconds, but it felt like an eternity.

The Sea Knight was hovering over the previous location of the ice floe. It was almost surreal, how much the landscape had changed. Minutes before, there had been a vast expanse of white. Now, all of that had been reduced to billions of tiny ice cubes, bobbing in the water.

In the distance, the Russians had abandoned their own helicopter. It had dropped into the frigid water and sunk from sight. Meanwhile, their submarine was no longer surrounded by the floe. It was now in the middle of the sea. Ivan was peeking through the hatch in the hull once again, watching our escape.

And Mike was nowhere to be seen.

I was seized by anguish, pain, and despair. I had known Mike for as long as I could remember. He had been a constant throughout every part of my life: kindergarten, elementary school, middle school, and ultimately spy school. And now he was gone.

I didn't want to believe it.

And so, even though it was dangerous and most likely pointless, I ran down the ramp at the rear of the helicopter, perched precariously on the edge, and looked toward the water, desperately hoping for some sign that Mike was still alive.

He was clinging to the very end of the ramp by his fingertips, dangling above the sea.

"Hey," he said with surprising composure, given the circumstances.

Relief and thrill and elation surged through me. "You're alive!" I yelled.

"I know," he replied. "But my fingers are really tired. Can you pull me up?"

I immediately dropped onto my belly, reached over the end of the ramp, and grabbed his arm. This was an incredibly dumb thing to do. Even if I hadn't just experienced how difficult it was to pull Svetlana out of the crevice, anyone with my math skills should have known there was a far better chance that Mike would drag me off the helicopter and into the sea than there was of me being able to pull him back into the helicopter. But I did it anyhow, because I couldn't bear the thought of doing nothing while my friend was in trouble.

And I was counting on my friends to have my back.

Which turned out to be the case.

Sure enough, Mike's weight started to pull me off the helicopter, but within seconds, Erica, Catherine, and Zoe were by my side. Together, all of us were able to pull Mike up and then hurriedly retreat into the safety of the helicopter.

After that, I threw my arms around Mike and held him tightly. "I'm so glad you're not dead."

"Me too," Mike replied.

Catherine gave Alexander a thumbs-up, signaling that everything was okay, and then Alexander brought the helicopter higher into the air.

It took a long time for the ramp to lift back into place, during which we could still see the ocean as it fell away beneath us and the submarine in the middle of it. Ivan had descended inside and sealed the hatch. The sub was sinking from view beneath the water.

It was only then, after our ordeal had finally ended, that I realized I was freezing.

I was soaked from all my time on the ice, and several snowballs' worth of slush had somehow made it into my clothing. Since the ramp was still partially open, frigid air was blasting into the helicopter. I was shivering uncontrollably.

Thankfully, there were plenty of warm blankets around for exactly this scenario. Svetlana and Cyrus were already swaddled in them. Erica quickly draped one over my shoulders.

"That was foolish," she told me.

"Mike didn't have much time left."

"You might have died along with him."

"But I didn't, thanks to you." I tried to smile at her, although it didn't quite work, since my teeth were chattering. It probably looked like I was trying to nibble on her.

She still got the idea and smiled back.

Zoe, Mike, and Catherine grabbed blankets as well.

"Holy cow," Mike said. "We almost got blown up like ten times out there, and then nearly got crushed by falling ice, and *then* I had to hang from a helicopter for dear life."

"Yes," Catherine agreed. "That was a rather harrowing experience."

"That was *amazing*," Mike said. "Everyone back at our

old middle school would be blown away if they saw what we just did."

"Only an amateur seeks glory in his deeds," Cyrus griped.

Catherine wheeled on him. "The reason Mike was hanging from the helicopter at all was because he saved *you*. So perhaps a 'thank you' is in order."

"I didn't need saving," Cyrus said defensively. "I can handle myself just fine." Then, before anyone could pressure him to apologize again, he shifted his attention to Svetlana, obviously looking to distract us from the fact that he'd needed to be saved. "What was all that about back there with your grandfather? What's your game here?"

"Game?" Svetlana asked blankly. "I have no game here."

"Don't pay any attention to him," Catherine said, looking mortified by Cyrus's behavior. "He's genetically incapable of being thankful. We owe you a great debt of gratitude for what you did for us. I know that couldn't have been easy."

"Stop coddling her!" Cyrus snapped, then glared at Svetlana again. "You really expect me to believe that you switched sides just now? That you turned your back on your own family, all of a sudden, just to save us? This is obviously a dastardly plot to place a mole in our operation."

Svetlana glared right back at him, stung by his words. "Yes, I turned my back on my family. But it was no plot. It broke my heart to do such a thing."

"Then why did you do it?" Zoe asked her.

Svetlana turned to her, looking surprisingly shy and awkward. "Is it not obvious? I thought you and I had a moment when we first met."

Zoe's eyes went wide in surprise. "You thought that too?"

"Yes," Svetlana replied. "It was very powerful to me."

"It was for me too!" Zoe exclaimed. "So that's why you came out here today? To see me?"

"Of course. And to prevent my grandfather from killing all of you if you had bad news for him."

"That was so sweet of you!" Zoe grinned broadly.

Svetlana returned the smile. "I am sorry that we had to meet under these circumstances. But I am still very pleased that it happened."

"Me too." Zoe suddenly shifted her attention to me. "I *told* you we had a moment! But you didn't believe me!"

"I just didn't want you to get your hopes up!" I said.

The rear ramp had finally shut. The interior of the helicopter was still cold, but at least there was no longer wind whipping through it. With my warm blanket, I was beginning to feel less like a popsicle and more like a human being.

Meanwhile, Cyrus seemed agitated by the entire situation. "This is all very sweet," he groused sarcastically, then jabbed a bony finger at Svetlana. "But the fact remains that your grandfather is an addlepated numbskull who can't handle the truth. We gave him what he asked for, and yet, he's still going to welch on the deal and set off his doomsday device. Which means we need to stop him. So what does he have planned?"

"I don't know," Svetlana replied.

"I don't believe you," Cyrus said.

"It's the truth." Svetlana lowered her eyes in shame. "He didn't trust me with that information. Even though I devoted my life to proving myself to him."

"You don't have any idea what Operation Doomsday is?" I asked worriedly.

"No."

"How about *where* it is?" Erica suggested.

"No."

"Do you have any snacks?" Alexander said.

"No," Svetlana replied, then paused and asked, "Snacks?"

"Action sequences make me hungry," Alexander explained. "And that one was a doozy. I'm famished. I thought I had a chocolate bar, but I can't remember what pocket I put it in." He glanced back at the rest of us from the cockpit. "Does anyone else have any food on them?"

"I've got a granola bar," I said, fishing it out of my utility belt, only to find that water had seeped in, reducing it to mush. "Although it's kind of soggy."

"Fine with me," Alexander said. "Once, on a mission in

Djibouti, I survived on nothing but raw earwigs for three days."

I brought him the limp granola bar. He happily tore open the wrapper and wolfed it down.

Cyrus resumed glaring at Svetlana. "You're not exactly contributing much to this mission. My team just risked a heck of a lot to save your life. . . ."

"We wouldn't even be *alive* if it wasn't for Svetlana," Zoe snapped heatedly. "She's contributed plenty."

Cyrus ignored her and kept his eyes locked on the Russian teen. "You honestly expect me to believe you don't know *anything* about Doomsday?"

Svetlana gulped nervously. "I know where we can find the plans."

"That's *good* news, isn't it?" Zoe asked her. "Why are you so concerned?"

"Because the plans are in Siberia," Svetlana replied.

Everyone else now gulped nervously. Even Cyrus.

"You mean we have to invade Russia to get them?" I asked.

"I'm afraid so," Svetlana answered.

INVASION

The Icebox

Inchoun Bay, Siberia

July 19 (Russian time)

2030 hours

Given that they are located on two different con-tinents, Alaska and Siberia are not very far apart. It is often noted that, at some points, the Bering Strait, which passes between the two countries, is only fifty miles wide—but the countries are even closer than that. In the middle of the strait are two islands, Big Diomede and Little Diomede, each of which is owned by a different country. The two of them are less than three miles apart; that's closer than Brooklyn is to New Jersey. Anyone with a good kayak and decent physical strength could paddle from the USA to Russia in less than an hour.

The FSB outpost we were headed to wasn't quite as adjacent to Alaska as Big Diomede, but it was still surprisingly close. It was situated on the northern flank of a forested peninsula that jutted into the Bering Strait. The Sea Knight could fly at 165 miles per hour, so it took us less than thirty minutes to get there from no-man's-land. Which was a bummer, because I had been hoping to nap on the way.

Bizarrely, since the international date line cuts between Russia and Alaska, even though our flight was brief, we landed a day later than we had left. It was already July nineteenth in Siberia, not July eighteenth.

The outpost was officially named Fort Chirikov, but according to Svetlana, everyone stationed there called it the Icebox. There were two reasons for this. First, the building was boxy in its design and located near the base of a glacier. Second, the heat rarely worked. "Even in summer, it is often cold enough to freeze your buttocks off," Svetlana explained. "Not exactly the most fun place to be stationed."

Despite the short flight, it was still going to take us quite a while to get to the Icebox, because we had to be stealthy in our approach. We didn't want the Russians to know we were coming. Even though it was late in the day, we were so far north that the sun never set at all in summer. At Svetlana's direction, Alexander landed the Sea Knight on the opposite side of a mountain several miles from the Icebox, where it wouldn't be seen. We would have to walk the rest of the way.

I was surprised that there wasn't more security along the Russian coast, like radar stations keeping an eye out for incoming aircraft, but Cyrus explained why this was the case. "Radar stations are really expensive, and Russia has over twenty thousand miles of coastline to monitor. Plus, there's not a whole lot out here worth protecting. It's just tundra and ice, and Moscow is over five thousand miles away. To be honest, most of Alaska isn't any better protected."

To further conceal our invasion, there was plenty of cloud cover. The weather was drastically different than it had been in the middle of the sea; a storm had parked itself along the coast, shrouding Siberia in dark, foreboding clouds. This helped shield us from sight as we illegally entered the country, but it also made our approach tricky. The helicopter was buffeted by powerful winds that shook us like a snow globe.

And once we landed, it was snowing.

It wasn't a blizzard. But still, it was snowing rather hard. In *July*.

The army had outfitted us with plenty of cold-weather gear, as dramatic shifts in climate were common in the Arctic. We had already ditched our damp clothes for dry ones en route; now we cinched all our zippers, buttons, and Velcro straps;

pulled on our muck boots; and headed out into the gloom.

Well, most of us did. Alexander stayed with the helicopter again. Although this time, Catherine made sure that the keys were left in the ignition and then tied them to the steering column with a bright pink ribbon to ensure that Alexander wouldn't misplace them again.

It was not an easy hike. In Siberia, as in Alaska, the summer was brief, the ground was wet, and the plants were designed for growing fast. Except for the rocky knoll that Alexander had found to land on, the boggy terrain was full of eight-foot-tall shrubs that probably hadn't even sprouted until a few weeks before. We had to hack through them with machetes that the army had lent us. It felt as though we were the first humans to ever come that way, which very well might have been the case. Except for the Icebox, the whole area appeared to be uninhabited.

By humans at least. There were certainly bears in the area. We kept finding evidence of grizzlies. Very large grizzlies. Paw prints as big as dinner plates in the damp earth, claw marks disturbingly high on trees—and large piles of, well . . . what bears were famous for doing in the woods.

The whole trip was so dour and arduous that even Catherine seemed grumpy. Meanwhile, Zoe and Svetlana were having a delightful time, excitedly getting to know each other and cheerfully oblivious to everything else. But while other young couples bonded over things like shared interests in books or movies or foods, Zoe and Svetlana were connecting over favorite martial arts styles and explosives.

"What's your favorite part of training to be a spy?" Zoe asked as we hacked our way through a swamp.

Svetlana considered that. "I most enjoy learning how to . . . how do you say? Kick other people's buttocks."

Zoe grinned. "That's my favorite part too! Although you're much better than me at it."

Svetlana blushed. "That is very nice of you to say. But I am not really that good."

"Are you kidding me? You're amazing! You were totally beating Erica in that fight at Fort King!"

"She was not," Erica said.

Zoe ignored her, focusing on Svetlana. "In fact, you probably would have beaten her if . . ."

". . . I hadn't seen you," Svetlana finished.

She and Zoe both laughed.

They went on like that for most of our slog, until we finally caught sight of the Icebox and all of us were forced to go silent unless communication was absolutely necessary. We paused at the top of a small, forested rise, from which we could observe our target.

On my last mission, I had encountered a supermax penitentiary, and even *that* had been more welcoming than the

Icebox. The Russian fortress wasn't ugly so much as bland: a dull gray cement cube. It looked as though no one had given the slightest thought to making it visually appealing. There were no decorative touches or hints of color. It was a building designed by someone with no imagination whatsoever.

Its surroundings didn't help. Somehow, the Icebox seemed to be situated in the most miserable spot on the entire Siberian coast. The woods we had been hiking through came to an abrupt end, and there was only lifeless rock ahead, with the exception of the occasional scraggly patch of tundra. The Icebox was built flush against the base of a squat and lumpy mountain, and a glacier zigzagged down from the peak to the fortress. Every other glacier I had seen was spectacular, but this one was gray and grimy, like an ice cube that had been dropped in the dirt. A dismal bay stretched in front of the Icebox; due to all the glacial silt, it had the murky hue of tarnished silver. With the leaden sky above, the entire landscape was bleak and colorless.

The area was also being patrolled by Russian guards. They were all gloomy and colorless as well.

There were only a few of them, which made sense, as a remote outpost like the Icebox probably didn't have a huge staffing budget. They wore heavy coats and thick boots to fend off the elements, but they still looked cold and grumpy as they trudged around the building.

"Do you think your grandfather has returned?" I asked Svetlana.

"No." She pointed to a concrete pier that jutted into the bay. "That's for the submarine. If it was back, we would see it docked there."

Mike grew concerned. "Then where is it? Do you think Ivan's gone off to trigger Doomsday already?"

"That is my fear," Svetlana confessed. "We must obtain my grandfather's plans as quickly as possible. I'll lead the way inside."

"Not so fast," Cyrus warned, then turned to the rest of us. "I'm not sure we can trust this girl. She's Ivan's granddaughter, and that whole family is nothing but a bunch of snakes. For all we know, this is one big setup, and she's leading us into a trap."

"As I recall, *you're* the one who led us into a trap of Ivan's," Zoe said indignantly. "Out on the ice today. Which we wouldn't have survived if it wasn't for Svetlana. So I trust her."

"Your vote doesn't count," Cyrus stated. "You've been making goo-goo eyes at her for the past three hours, so you're obviously emotionally compromised."

Zoe bridled and started to say something that I presumed would be nasty, but Catherine spoke up first. "Cyrus, since you brought up the idea of a vote, let's take one. All in favor of trusting Svetlana?" She raised her hand.

So did Erica, Mike, and I. Zoe defiantly held hers up as well.

"It's decided, then," Catherine announced. "Svetlana, tell us what to do."

While Cyrus glowered, Svetlana led us deeper into the cover of the forest and sketched out a plan of the Icebox in the mucky ground. The layout wasn't very complicated. A mess hall, a few offices, and some bunk rooms were arranged around a more secure central office where Ivan kept his plans locked in a safe. The front entrance was protected by thick steel doors that could be braced inside with a crossbar, like those on a medieval castle, and the entire building backed into the rocky flank of the mountain. It appeared that getting inside was hopeless.

Except for the secret entrance that Svetlana knew about.

"There is an escape tunnel through the mountain," she explained. "In case the Icebox ever came under attack. And since the tunnel's existence is classified, the entrance to it is not nearly as well guarded as the front doors of the Icebox."

"Sounds like a good way in," Mike said. "Where is it?"

"I will show you," Svetlana replied.

Cyrus started to question this, but Catherine immediately cut him off. "We voted. You lost. If you don't like the plan, you can go wait with Alexander in the helicopter."

"No," Cyrus grumped. "I'll stay."

With that decided, Svetlana led our assault. Catherine

insisted that weapons were only to be used as a last resort; we were to take out our enemies with chloroform-soaked rags. Mike and I brought up the rear, as our combat skills weren't quite as good as everyone else's, although we were still prepared for battle.

And then we infiltrated the Icebox.

It was surprisingly easy.

It wasn't *really* easy, as there were still enemy guards to overpower and steel doors to get through, but it was ultimately far easier than any of our classes in infiltration and incapacitating enemies had led us to expect it would be.

For example, in Advanced Infiltration, our practical exams always involved trying to slip past guards who were expecting an attack at any moment. They were never real guards, of course. They were students or professors *pretending* to be guards, and they were highly alert for any sign of trouble. Sneaking up on them was nearly impossible.

Meanwhile, the guards around the Icebox were bored out of their skulls. No enemy had ever attacked the Icebox, and the guards probably felt no one was ever going to. It was a dingy outpost at the farthest end of Russia, and it was unlikely that anyone knew Ivan had stashed anything of importance there. According to Svetlana, even in the Russian Army, which was famed for hardship and misery, protecting the Icebox was considered a terrible job, and so no one wanted to do it. With no volunteers, the Russians had to ship out men against their will, usually soldiers who were so incompetent that their commanders wanted to get rid of them. All of them hated the Icebox and regarded each patrol mission as a punishment, rather than a duty. Not one was on the alert as we approached. Most were doing what bored people anywhere else in the world would be doing: looking at their phones.

The first guard we came across was sullenly sitting on a rock, playing Flapjack Frenzy. The next was reading his email, and the one after that was trying to talk to his girlfriend and complaining about the terrible reception. He was so noisy and distracted that he didn't even notice when Mike accidentally stepped on a twig and made it crack like a gunshot. It was possible that the guy wouldn't have even spotted a battalion of tanks approaching. A fourth guard was actually patrolling, rather than looking at his phone. However, he was so miserable, trudging about in the cold, that he looked thankful when he realized that he was being knocked unconscious.

It was all so easy that even I was allowed a turn. The fifth guard we came across was stationed directly outside the secret door to the escape tunnel, and he was so uninterested in his job that he had fallen asleep. He was seated on a rock, leaning back against the mountain, snoring soundly. I simply tiptoed up to him and clapped a chloroformed rag over his face. He immediately woke in surprise, but was so groggy that he only managed a feeble attempt to fend me off. It was like being attacked by a sloth. He took a swipe at me in slow motion, but halfway through, his eyes drooped and he sagged back down again.

Erica looked at me expectantly. "What'd you think of your first time knocking someone out? Fun, right?"

"It was a little anticlimactic," I said honestly.

"Yeah. It's more exciting when they struggle a bit. But still, nice work." Erica gave me a playful jab in the shoulder. "Now let's blow the secret door."

This part wasn't that difficult either, since Catherine and Erica had explosives in their utility belts and were skilled with them—and Svetlana knew precisely where they needed to be placed to open the secret entrance to the tunnel. Catherine and Erica used exactly the right amount, which blasted off the lock without making much noise, and then the door swung open.

The hinges creaked balefully, but there was no other sound.

"It's not alarmed?" Mike asked, surprised.

"What's the point of alarming a secret door?" Svetlana replied. "No one's supposed to know about it, and alarms cost money. There are no motion sensors or grids of lasers in the tunnel either. It's just a tunnel."

"This would have been so much harder without you," Zoe told her thankfully. "I'm really glad you switched sides."

"Me too," Svetlana said, and then they giggled a bit.

The rest of our way into the Icebox was equally uneventful. Without booby traps, the tunnel was simple to negotiate. The door that led into the fortress wasn't even locked. The remaining soldiers were all asleep in their bunks; after all, it was now nearly midnight. There were only seven of them, one for each of us, so we each took a chloroformed rag, positioned ourselves beside our target, and rendered them unconscious in sync.

Ivan's central office was secured with a padlock that Erica could have picked within seconds, but Svetlana already knew the combination. The office was furnished with a cheap old desk and some plastic folding chairs. The crude shelves held ratty paperback books that appeared to have been read several hundred times, a chessboard with handmade pieces whittled from driftwood, and a tremendous amount of vodka. A large map of the world dominated one wall, while on the opposite side of the room was a portrait of Joseph Stalin; both appeared to have been there since World War II. Concealed behind the portrait, an ancient steel safe was built into the wall.

"I don't know the combination to this one," Svetlana admitted apologetically. "Can any of you crack it?"

"I could've done this in kindergarten," Erica said, then pressed an ear to the side and twisted the dial. "This shouldn't take more than a minute or two."

Mike said, "It's about time something on one of our missions actually went well."

"Shhh!" Zoe hissed. "Are you crazy? You've violating Twomey's Rule of Premature Gloating!"

"What is that?" Svetlana asked curiously.

Zoe answered, "You can't say that you've gotten out of a situation *before* you've gotten out of it—or you'll jinx it."

Svetlana laughed. "You're superstitious?"

"No," Zoe said, growing embarrassed. "I'm practical. You don't want to drop your guard before a mission is over." She wheeled on Mike. "Like this doofus is doing."

"I didn't violate the rule!" Mike protested. "All I'm saying is every time we do *anything* on a mission, it always goes sideways. So it's nice to not have that happen for once."

"Shhh!" Zoe hissed again. "Shut your piehole!"

"Relax," Mike told her. "I'm not jinxing anything."

At that moment, Erica figured out the last bit of the combination. There was a click, and then the safe's door swung open.

The only thing inside was an old leather-bound notebook.

"My grandfather's secret file!" Svetlana pronounced. "We've got it!"

Mike snatched the notebook out of the safe. "See?" he said to Zoe. "Everything's perfectly fine."

At which point, everything promptly went wrong.

BOOBY TRAP

The Icebox

Inchoun Bay, Siberia

July 20 (Russian time)

0030 hours

There was a monofilament wire attached to Ivan's notebook, so thin that it was almost invisible. Mike certainly didn't see it as he yanked the notebook out of the safe.

But we all *heard* it. First, there was a soft twang as the wire pulled taut. And then there was a louder clank from deep inside the safe as some machinery engaged.

"Get down!" Erica yelled while simultaneously tackling Mike.

Catherine had the exact same reaction, except she tackled me, while Svetlana tackled Zoe.

Cyrus simply dove to the floor alone, although his reaction time was a fraction of a second slower than the others'.

A thick jet of flame blasted out of the safe, so powerful that it crossed the entire room and set the map on the far wall on fire. Apparently, Ivan had rigged a souped-up flamethrower to his safe to flambé anyone who tried to steal his notebook.

The flame flared for fifteen seconds, and then the gas supply coughed and gave out.

"Whoa!" Mike gasped. "We nearly got charbroiled!"

"Some of us *did*." Cyrus got back up off the floor, revealing that all the hair had been cooked off the top of his head, leaving him with the tonsure of a Franciscan friar. His scalp was now bald as a cue ball, except for a thin halo of slightly singed hair. He was exceptionally unhappy about this, and his head was smoking from the attack, which left him looking like a cartoon character who had literally blown their top. "You ruined my hair!" he screamed at Mike.

"Me?" Mike asked, offended. "Ivan did that to you! This was *his* booby trap!"

There were more clanks from the wall behind the safe. More machinery was engaging. And we didn't want to stick around to see what any of it would do.

We bolted for the office door. Behind us, there was a loud hiss, and green gas that I could only assume was poisonous began to seep out of the safe.

This was followed by several large blasts. Although they sounded as if they had detonated outside the Icebox, far away from us.

"What do you think those were?" Mike asked worriedly as all of us raced to the front doors of the fortress. Since we had snuck in through the secret tunnel, the doors were still braced with the crossbar to prevent intruders from entering.

"Maybe it was some other booby trap detonating prematurely by mistake?" Zoe suggested hopefully.

"My grandfather does not make mistakes," Svetlana said gravely.

We all lifted the crossbar out of its resting slot and let it clatter to the floor. Then Catherine quickly unlatched the doors and flung them open.

"Then what do you think those blasts were?" I asked Svetlana.

We ran out of the fortress. Despite the late hour, we were so far north that the sun hadn't set; it was just lurking on the horizon, casting a dim, dreary light.

A rumbling noise from high above stopped us in our tracks.

We spun around and looked at the mountain that loomed over the Icebox.

"I'd say it was several explosive charges triggering a rock-slide," Svetlana replied.

Sure enough, the side of the mountain was coming apart before our eyes. Boulders the size of small homes had broken loose and were tumbling toward us. Each was so big that, as it rolled, it knocked hundreds of other rocks free. Those joined the flow, hurtling our way.

"We can't outrun that!" I yelled to the others. "We have to double back!"

No one questioned my math. We fled back into the Icebox.

A second later, the first boulders arrived. They pounded on the roof and then thudded to the ground where we had just stood. More rocks then fell atop those, landing with such force that they were pulverized into rubble. Then came yet more rocks, along with several hundred tons of dirt and debris. Within seconds, the entrance to the building was buried deep in earth and stone.

The Icebox might not have been designed for beauty, but it was sturdy enough to remain standing. Which was most likely the point of Ivan's booby trap. He didn't want to kill his own men; he only wanted to kill anyone who tried to steal his notebook. If a thief tried to run, they would be flattened by the landslide; if they came back into the Icebox, they'd be trapped with a whole lot of angry Russians.

But Ivan hadn't counted on us sneaking in through the back door and preemptively knocking all the Russians unconscious. So we only had the poisonous gas to contend with.

Thankfully, the gas was slow-moving and had stayed relatively contained. (Because, once again, Ivan didn't want to kill his own men.) And yet, the cloud of it was still slowly emerging from Ivan's office, like a fog rolling in. Since it was a bilious green, it was easy to see, and we skirted around it while holding our breath as we cut back through the Icebox to the secret tunnel.

Once we were clear of the gas, Mike asked Svetlana, "Is that it for the booby traps?"

"How should I know?" Svetlana asked.

"You're Ivan's granddaughter!" Mike replied. "You know what kind of guy he is. Do you think he rigged the escape tunnel with traps as well? I don't want to run into a gauntlet of rotating knives or fall into a pool full of sharks."

Everyone realized that Mike had a good point. We all paused as we reached the entrance to the escape tunnel and looked to Svetlana expectantly.

"I don't think there is going to be a pool full of sharks in a tunnel in Siberia," she said.

"Mike might be exaggerating, but it's still worth considering," Zoe told her. "What's the chance that Ivan rigged the tunnel as well?"

Svetlana thought for a moment, then said, "I don't think Ivan would have done that. He would have left a way out for himself and his agents—and me, if I was visiting. He probably figured the flamethrower, the poison gas, and the rockslide were enough booby traps to take care of any thieves."

"You're sure?" Catherine asked.

"Ninety-nine percent sure. Not a hundred."

We all looked at one another for a moment.

"I think we need to risk those odds," Erica said finally. "It's better than staying here until the Russians wake up again."

"Or the poisonous gas reaches us," I added.

"Agreed," Cyrus said. "Though I say we make Mike go through the tunnel first. Since he started all this trouble."

"Cyrus!" Catherine exclaimed. "He's still just a trainee. And you're the team leader."

"He cost me my hair!" Cyrus cried accusingly.

"Fine. I'll lead the way," Catherine said. And before Cyrus could protest, she ducked past him into the tunnel.

The rest of us followed her. Ahead of us, Catherine moved briskly and confidently, trusting Svetlana's assessment. On the other hand, I was terrified that something else was going to go wrong any second. I didn't expect a pool full of sharks—although Ivan seemed like the sort of person who would have at least considered the idea, and possibly even hired an evil marine biologist to look into it—but I figured there could definitely be another trap or two. So it was a huge relief when we made it through the tunnel without encountering any spikes erupting from the floor or jets of flesh-eating acid or giant boulders that rolled down ramps and flattened us into crepes. Instead, we emerged safely into the fresh air.

The guard that I had chloroformed earlier was still dozing peacefully by the entrance, despite the fact that a massive rockslide had occurred close by. Quite a bit of rubble had fallen on the guard, leaving him partially buried, and yet he remained fast asleep.

"You really knocked him out well," Erica observed, seeming impressed.

"Thanks," I said, and then gasped in surprise.

I had just noticed the full result of the landslide that Ivan's booby trap had triggered.

It was much bigger than I had expected. A significant section of the mountain and the glacier had been forcibly relocated, transforming the entire landscape. The Icebox had vanished from sight. Now, it was buried beneath an enormous pile of rock and ice, which spread from the base of the mountain all the way into the bay. In fact, it went so far into the water that it had created a brand-new peninsula. I had been correct in my assessment that we couldn't have run for it. If we had tried, we would have been crushed and entombed within seconds.

Everyone else seemed equally stunned by the extent of the damage—except Cyrus, who swiped the woolen hat from the unconscious guard, pulled it down tight over his own head to hide his newly bald pate, and then radioed Alexander. "Fledgling, this is Eagle. It's time to fly."

"He should probably change his code name to Bald Eagle," Mike whispered, provoking giggles from Zoe and Svetlana.

Alexander came on the radio a few seconds later. "I'm on my way. And I thought we said my code name was going to be Alpha Dog."

"I never agreed to that, Fledgling," Cyrus replied. "Now stop crying and start flying."

Alexander sighed meekly. "Okay."

Mike was still carrying Ivan's notebook.

Catherine plucked it from his hands and flipped it open. With all the booby traps, there hadn't been a moment to look at it until now. Catherine took once glance at the first page and groaned. "Oh for goodness' sake."

Erica looked at her, concerned. "What's wrong, Mom?"

"It's in code." Catherine held the notebook out for us to see.

Sure enough, everything on the page was encrypted. I

could tell this even without knowing Russian, because Ivan had written in numbers, rather than letters. It looked to be a particularly tricky code to decipher. There weren't even breaks to indicate spaces between words. Instead, the entire page was filled with a continuous stream of digits.

Cyrus gave Svetlana a challenging look. "Tell me you know how to decode this."

Svetlana cringed. "Sorry. No."

"Great," Cyrus spat. "Some help you are."

"Some help?" Zoe repeated, flushing angrily. "She saved our lives on the ice and got us in and out of the Icebox alive. If it wasn't for her, we'd have nothing at all!"

"We *do* have nothing!" Cyrus yelled back. "If we can't translate this notebook, it's useless!"

"There's no point in losing faith yet," Catherine told him sharply. "Give it to Benjamin and let him see what he can do. . . ."

"Why Ben?" Cyrus asked sharply. "Erica's got more decoding skill than he does."

"Yes, but I need her help to defeat the Russians," Catherine said. "They seem to have woken up again."

Sure enough, the remaining Russian guards who everyone had knocked out before entering the Icebox were no longer unconscious. And now they were on the alert and aware that we were trouble. All of them were racing across the rubble field left by the landslide, aiming weapons at us, and yelling angrily.

"Great," Cyrus grumbled, then roughly shoved the notebook into my hands. "Don't lose that. And keep your head down." He shifted his annoyed gaze to Mike. "You stay with him. You've done enough damage today."

With that, he joined Catherine, Erica, Zoe, and Svetlana as they raced into action.

Mike and I dropped behind the cover of a large rock that had, until recently, been located several hundred yards up the mountain, and went to work examining the code.

Cyrus was right that Erica had better decoding skills than I did, but Mike and I had been boning up on codes and ciphers over the past few weeks, so there was a chance we could at least figure something out.

"Hmmm," Mike said thoughtfully, looking over the rows of numbers. "He uses all ten digits, so it's not a binary recursion code."

"It could be a Zimmerman square," I suggested.

"Yeah, that's what I was thinking."

From a few feet away came the guttural grunting of two people fighting, followed by the distinct, high-pitched squeak of a large Russian agent who had just been kicked in the soft bits.

"The problem is," I said, "there's over a trillion possibilities of arranging those ten digits on a Zimmerman square."

"So?" Mike asked. "You're a math genius."

"I'd still need a supercomputer to run all the possibilities. And that's assuming this *is* a Zimmerman square in the first place. It could be a false Zimmerman. Or a Duplicitous Decagram. Or something we've never seen before."

A Russian war cry rang out nearby, although it segued very abruptly into a sudden, sharp wail of pain, followed by abundant whimpering.

Mike scrutinized the notebook even harder. "Could this be a Watusi Wingnut? Or a Disputin' Rasputin? Or a Black Hole of Calcutta? All those use ten digits."

"Yeah, it could be any of those. Or it could be a mega-amalgamation of them."

"If that's the case, it'll take us thirty years to crack this."

"If we're lucky."

There was a distant shriek of agony, and then the thud of someone collapsing heavily on the ground.

After that, I heard the whirr of an incoming helicopter.

Cyrus rounded the boulder Mike and I had been hunkered behind, wiping what looked like someone else's blood off his sleeve. "The enemy is neutralized," he reported. "Have you solved the code yet?"

"We've only had ninety seconds," I replied. "We haven't even figured out what kind of code it *is* yet."

Cyrus huffed with annoyance. "While you've been slacking off over here, I got one of Ivan's guys to cough up some information. Operation Doomsday goes off at noon today."

"That's in less than twelve hours!" I exclaimed.

"I know," Cyrus said flatly. "So crack the dang code, or we're screwed."

DECRYPTION

Tuckernuck Military Refueling Depot

Kotzebue, Alaska

July 19 (back on American time)

0600 hours

Decryption isn't easy.

As evidence, consider that the entire Central Intelligence Agency hasn't been able to solve a code that has been at its own headquarters for several decades.

The code is called Kryptos, and it is publicly displayed on a sculpture of the same name. It was commissioned by the CIA from a Maryland sculptor named Jim Sanborn, who unveiled it in 1990, and it sits in a courtyard right next to the main cafeteria. *Kryptos* is a wavy wall of copper that is twenty feet long and twelve feet high. A code is carved into it: 865 letters, along with four question marks. Back before the unveiling, the CIA circulated a memo suggesting that perhaps its own employees should have a head start solving the puzzle before the general public got a crack at it. It was presumed that two days ought to be good enough.

More than thirty years later, they still haven't solved the puzzle.

Then again, no one else has either. Not the best cryptographers from the FSB, MI6, the Mossad, or any other intelligence agency. Or any of the thousands of professional and amateur decoding specialists. Even with Jim Sanborn occasionally giving hints.

Remember, Jim Sanborn is not a professional coding specialist. Or a puzzler creator. He's a sculptor. And yet his 865 letters have flummoxed the entire world for over a generation.

Luckily, Ivan Shumovsky's code wasn't quite that complicated.

Which made sense. Anyone keeping a coded journal, like Ivan did, wouldn't want to use an intensely complicated code, as it would make the act of writing things down—or converting them back to something readable again—too grueling.

But it was still complex enough that it was a bear to crack.

It took our whole team hours to do it, requiring my math skills; Catherine's, Cyrus's, Erica's, and Zoe's decryption skills; and—most importantly—Svetlana's knowledge of her grandfather. (Mike made us all snacks, while Alexander flew the helicopter.) The difficulty of deciphering Ivan's notebook was compounded by the fact that we were all exhausted. Each of us kept nodding off. Finally, Catherine arranged for a rotating napping schedule so that at least a few people could be working on the code at any time while the others recharged.

We struggled with the code throughout the entire flight back across the Bering Sea to Western Alaska. We didn't want to head all the way back to Toksook, where we'd borrowed the helicopter, because it was quite far south; the last time we'd seen Ivan, he'd been pretty far north, indicating that his doomsday device was located in that direction. Plus, the helicopter had burned plenty of fuel, so we headed to the Tuckernuck Military Refueling Depot in Kotzebue.

Kotzebue was the county seat of the Northwest Arctic Borough of Alaska, which was one of the most sparsely populated places on earth. Despite being the same size as the state of Virginia, less than eight thousand people lived there. Kotzebue was the second-largest community in the United States north of the Arctic Circle, but its entire population could have easily fit inside a middle school gymnasium.

The town was located on a gravel spit at the end of a

peninsula that jutted into Kotzebue Sound. It was as flat as a pancake and only a few square blocks. The local airport was actually bigger than the town itself.

The Tuckernuck Fuel Depot was located at the airport. There were stations like this all through the arctic, especially along the western coast of Alaska. The US had been sending surveillance planes to spy on Russia since the 1950s, and the less distance they had to travel to refuel, the better. It helped that Western Alaska had plenty of oil. In some places, the military could drill it out, refine it, and pump it all within the same facility.

Tuckernuck was a small depot: four gas pumps and two Quonset huts. Only a dozen people were stationed there. One hut served as the bunkhouse; the other served as everything else: the mess hall, offices, radar station, and armory. A cold wind was whipping across the tarmac, making the Quonsets tremble like Jell-O.

It took a while for Cyrus and Alexander to explain what two CIA agents, an MI6 agent, and a handful of teenagers were doing with a US military helicopter—and even more time to get permission to refuel it. While this happened, the rest of us headed off to the Quonset hut that served as the mess hall to get what was either an early breakfast or an exceptionally late dinner. Or possibly, it was lunch. With the permanent daylight and the fact that we had hopped the international date line twice in the past day, even I was having trouble keeping track of what time it was.

Due to the weirdness of the international date line, even though we had left Siberia on July twentieth, we landed in America on July nineteenth, approximately twenty-one hours *before* we had taken off. It was confusing enough to make my head hurt, and I already had Ivan's code to contend with, so I tried to focus on that instead, as well as not passing out in my meal. Despite the brief naps, I was still tired. We all were, but we had to press on anyhow. Twice, I nodded off and ended up facedown in my waffles.

Finally, our teamwork paid off. Svetlana revealed that Ivan had once had a beloved Siberian husky named Poludnitsa, and that name turned out to be the code key for a ten-digit daisy chain with a St. Petersburg encryption shift. That cracked the code wide open, which was cause for celebration—although our work wasn't done yet. Not by a long shot.

We still had to translate everything from the code into Russian, which Svetlana then translated into English. And there was a great deal to translate. Ivan had filled the pages of his notebook from top to bottom, and then scribbled in the margins as well, as though paper was a rare commodity in Siberia and he didn't want to waste one square millimeter of it. We tore the notebook apart, divvied up the sections, and each set to work breaking down Ivan's writings.

It turned out, a lot of it was useless.

Ivan's obsession with the idea that the United States had stolen Alaska from Russia turned out to be far more severe than even Cyrus had realized. The notebook was filled with dozens of misguided theories about how it might have happened, along with accusations of hundreds of other bizarre crimes. Ivan suspected American agents of doing everything from infecting the explorer Vitus Bering with scurvy to training humpback whales to ram Russian submarines. In addition, much of what he had written was mere ranting. The phrases *Death to the USA* and *Mother Russia will rise again* appeared over and over again.

It was all very embarrassing for Svetlana. "It seems that my grandfather might need some therapy," she observed.

Zoe patted her hand reassuringly. "If you shake anyone's family tree, a few nuts are going to fall out."

"But your family members aren't plotting a doomsday attack on another country, are they?" Svetlana asked.

"Er . . . no," Zoe admitted. "Although one time, my grandmother assaulted a random man on the street with her umbrella because she mistakenly thought he'd stolen a candy bar from her. She got arrested by the police and everything. It turned out the candy bar was in her purse the whole time."

"That's not nearly as bad as what my grandfather seems to be plotting." Svetlana sighed sadly. "And I fear I am partly to blame for this. I should never have supported him."

"Oh, you're definitely partly to blame," Erica agreed.

"Erica!" Catherine exclaimed, now looking embarrassed by *her* family. "That's no way to talk to our guest."

"Until two days ago, she was working with Ivan," Erica argued. "When we first met, she attacked me."

"And you attacked *her*," Catherine said. "Both of you come from families that have been in the spy business for a very long time. And both of you have grandfathers who can be a little"—she glanced at Cyrus to confirm that he was napping on a cot nearby before continuing her thought—"set in their ways where their enemies are concerned. You've done plenty for Cyrus without questioning it."

"Cyrus might be crotchety," Erica countered, "but he's not a lunatic."

"Erica!" Catherine exclaimed again.

"It's okay," Svetlana said. "I see now that my grandfather *does* have some issues." She shifted her attention to Erica. "But you must realize, for most of my life, I was only exposed to one side of the story: *his*. He kept me in the dark about many things and convinced me that all Americans were wicked."

"When did you realize that wasn't true?" Zoe asked.

Svetlana looked into her eyes. "When I first saw *you*. You were American, and I knew that you couldn't possibly be evil. So I started to wonder if anything else Ivan had told me was a lie. And then, when he began plotting to blow up the ice floe with you on it, I knew I couldn't let that happen. I played along, pretending to be a good granddaughter, and hoping that Ivan would come to his senses and realize what he was doing was wrong. Sadly, he did not . . . and now I am the shame of the Shumovsky family." She broke her gaze with Zoe and turned away.

Zoe clutched her hand. "It's your grandfather who should be ashamed of his actions, not you. He's the one plotting doomsday. You're trying to stop him!"

"Speaking of which, has anyone found *anything* yet?" Mike asked.

"I think I might have," I said. Svetlana had taught us all the term Ivan used to refer to Doomsday in Russian—konets sveta—and I had come across it that very moment. I slid my pages of decryption across the table to Svetlana, who glanced at the Russian I had written out so far and then stiffened in excitement.

"I think this is it!" she announced, then quickly skimmed through the rest. As she read on, her excitement at finally discovering the section on Doomsday faded, and her face creased with concern.

Erica and Catherine both read the pages over her shoulder and grew visibly worried as well.

"What's wrong?" Mike asked.

"Wake Cyrus," Catherine told us. "And get Alexander. I only want to explain all this once."

Mike leapt to his feet and raced off to find Alexander, sticking me with rousing Cyrus, who could be even more irritable than usual right after he'd been woken. The others set about translating the rest of Ivan's code to get the full scope of his plans.

Cyrus must have been exhausted, because he didn't wake up when I shook him gently. Instead, he kept snoring loud enough to knock the paint off the walls. I had to kneel beside him and bark, "Cyrus! Wake up!"

His eyes snapped open, and then he sprang to his feet, grabbed me by the shirt and slammed me against the wall.

"Cyrus! It's me!" I shouted.

Cyrus paused in the process of cocking a fist back and blinked the sleep from his eyes. "Dang it, Benjamin. I thought you were Ivan!"

"Why would Ivan tell you to wake up? Wouldn't he just attack you in your sleep?"

"I don't presume to know what that madman would do." Cyrus released me but didn't bother to apologize. Instead, he still seemed annoyed at me. "What's the point of interrupting my shut-eye?"

"We found something in Ivan's notebook."

Cyrus spun around and hurried to the table where the

decryption was underway. At the same time, Mike came through the door with Alexander in tow.

"What's the news?" Alexander asked.

Catherine looked up from the notebook. "We've figured out what Ivan's doomsday plan is." She paused dramatically, then announced, "He's plotting to blow up the oil reserves in the Arctic National Wildlife Refuge."

"What's that?" Mike asked.

"It's a wildlife refuge in northeastern Alaska," Erica explained. "It's a critical breeding ground for migratory birds, caribou, polar bears, and musk ox."

"It also holds the largest untapped reserve of oil in the United States," Zoe continued. "But while a few exploratory wells have been dug, drilling has been placed on hold due to environmental concerns."

"Which leaves an estimated *half a trillion* gallons of crude underground," Catherine went on. "And Ivan has hidden a device that will ignite it all somewhere in the refuge."

"Where?" I asked.

"He doesn't say," Catherine noted. "But he plans to detonate the device by firing a short-range sea-to-surface missile at it from his submarine. That must be where he's heading right now. We need to act immediately if we're going to stop him."

"Then let's go!" Alexander exclaimed. "The chopper's fueled up and ready to fly!"

We all leapt to our feet and headed for the door, only to find Cyrus blocking our path. He had his hands on his hips and a stern scowl on his face.

"Not so fast," he said. "We're not going anywhere."

PROTECTION

Tuckernuck Military Refueling Depot

Kotzebue, Alaska

July 19

0630 hours

The rest of us froze in surprise, thrown by Cyrus's declaration and struggling to comprehend what was going on.

"What are you doing?" Mike exclaimed. "Are you in cahoots with Ivan?"

Cyrus recoiled as though he'd been slapped. "Of course I'm not in cahoots with that dunderhead!"

"Then why are you preventing us from stopping his plans?" I asked.

"Because his plans are ridiculous!" Cyrus crowed. "Which is why we don't *need* to stop them."

The rest of us looked to one another to see if anyone was following Cyrus's logic. Even Erica appeared perplexed.

"Grandpa," she said. "There are half a trillion gallons of oil in the ANWR. If Ivan blows that up, it will create an absolutely massive explosion."

"In the least populated portion of the entire United States!" Cyrus added, then burst into laughter. "Almost no one lives up there!"

"But *some* people do," Zoe protested.

"A few hundred, tops," Cyrus replied dismissively.

"And you're okay with losing them?" Mike demanded.

Cyrus gave him the stink eye. "I'm not okay with losing *anyone*. But the people I care about most are in this room. The chances of us stopping this ludicrous scheme before Ivan sets it in motion are infinitesimal. There's no way I'm letting this team race off to ground zero for odds like that. Sometimes, in this business, you have to make a calculated decision based on the facts."

"Well here's another fact for you," Erica announced. "There are many more lives at stake in the refuge than just the human ones. There's nearly a million caribou, for starters."

"Caribou?" Cyrus snorted with disdain. "I'm not letting you put your life on the line for a bunch of weird antelope."

Erica flushed angrily. "Caribou are *not* weird! They're fascinating creatures, and they deserve our protection!"

"I know you've got a soft spot for animals," Cyrus told her. "But you have to think rationally here."

Zoe and Mike now appeared just as surprised by this exchange as they were by Cyrus's interfering with our mission.

"Erica has a soft spot for animals?" Mike whispered to me. "Since when?"

"Okay," Catherine said to Cyrus. "Let's think rationally. There are far more lives at stake here than the ones in the wildlife refuge. Igniting all that fuel at once will release a devastating amount of heat into our atmosphere, triggering a cataclysmic series of events. It will greatly exacerbate the effects of global warming, throwing our entire planet into chaos."

Cyrus gave another snort. "Don't start with me on all that liberal hooey about climate change."

"It's not hooey!" Svetlana held up the pages of Ivan's notebook we had translated. "It's a key part of my grandfather's plan. If the world gets warmer, which country benefits the most?"

"Russia?" I guessed.

"Exactly," Svetlana said. "Right now, most of Russia is really, really cold. But that would change. If the planet warms, Russia gets more farmland. If the ice in the Arctic melts, Russia gets more coastline. My grandfather and other high-ranking Russians have been seeking ways to make this happen for years. Now, it appears they have found one."

Catherine jumped in. "Meanwhile, tropical cities will become unbearably hot, temperate farmland will become unusable, and entire ecosystems will collapse. The lives of billions of people will be threatened."

Cyrus shook his head. "None of that's gonna happen. Like I said, Ivan's plan is outrageous. For all we know, this doomsday device of his won't even work. But it still might be dangerous. Going up there to try to stop it is a suicide mission. Let's wait until after Ivan's knuckleheaded attack, and then—if he hasn't blown himself up by accident—we call in the navy and have them blast his submarine out of the water. After all, he'll have committed an act of war against us, so we'll be allowed to retaliate."

Svetlana bit her lip. Even though she had cut ties with Ivan, she seemed concerned about him dying.

I was worried too. On the one hand, I didn't want to go on a suicide mission. But on the other, it seemed wrong to let such a destructive event occur without even trying to stop it. I didn't want innocent humans—or caribou or polar bears or migrating birds—to die. And while Cyrus didn't seem to believe in the potential disastrous climactic effects, I certainly did.

The rest of the team looked worried as well. We all turned to Catherine for guidance.

"I appreciate your concern for us," she informed Cyrus. "But this isn't your call. It's all of ours. Now, I'm heading north to stop Ivan. If you want to sit this one out, you're welcome to. Anyone else who wants to come is welcome to join me." With that, she stormed past Cyrus and headed for the door.

Erica joined her without a moment's hesitation. Zoe, Svetlana, Mike, and I all wavered, then followed them.

"Catherine!" Cyrus called. "If you want to put your life on the line, that's fine. But I can't allow you to put my grand-daughter's or the rest of those kids' lives in jeopardy!"

"They've made their choice," Catherine told him. "You can't stop us."

"Actually, I can," Cyrus said.

Catherine barged through the door onto the tarmac—and then froze in surprise.

All twelve of the soldiers stationed at the depot now stood between us and the helicopter. Each was pointing a gun at us.

Erica wheeled on her grandfather. "You've undermined us!"

"No. I'm *protecting* you," Cyrus insisted. "And I'm prepared to go even further if I have to. So why don't all of you stand down before this gets messy?"

"You're bluffing," Catherine challenged.

"I'm not," Cyrus said.

"Let's see about that." Catherine continued onward toward the helicopter. So did Erica, Svetlana, Zoe, Mike, and I.

But not Alexander.

Erica turned back to him. "Why aren't you coming?"

"Er . . . ," Alexander said weakly. "This *really* does seem like a suicide mission."

All of us stopped in our tracks again.

Catherine gave Alexander a look of betrayal. "Alexander, we need you to fly that helicopter."

"I know," Alexander said, seeming very anxious about this entire conversation. "And I hate to say this, but I agree with Dad. This is a bad idea."

"You're the king of bad ideas!" Erica protested.

"Which is why I'm so good at recognizing them," Alexander concluded. "Now, I know that all of you make a very impressive team—and I have a tremendous amount of faith in you. But I can't fly my wife and daughter, who I love dearly—and the rest of you kids, who I care about very much—into something as dangerous as this. I'm sorry."

"I'll say you're sorry," Erica snapped. "I guess *I'll* just have to fly the helicopter. Come on, everyone." She headed toward the helicopter, ignoring the soldiers stationed in front of her.

Cyrus withdrew a sedation gun from his utility belt and fired a dart into Erica's rear end. Then he shot Catherine, too.

Both of the Hale women turned back to him, stunned. Erica looked like she wanted to leap into action, but the sedative was acting too quickly. Her eyes were already drooping. "You're the worst grandfather in the worlllllldpthhhmmmm," she told Cyrus, although she passed out in the middle of the thought and pitched forward.

I caught her before she could hit the tarmac.

Mike caught Catherine as she slumped.

"I told you this would get messy," Cyrus said to us, then whistled to the soldiers. "Lock these folks up and make sure they don't cause any trouble," he ordered.

The soldiers came across the tarmac toward us, keeping us at gunpoint.

"You can't do this!" I yelled at Cyrus. "You're playing right into Ivan's hands!"

"No, Ivan's playing right into mine," he declared. "Setting off this absurd doomsday device is gonna give me all the leverage I need to take him out for good. I know you're upset now, but trust me, by this time tomorrow, you'll see I've made the right decision. Ivan won't be around to cause us any more trouble."

Zoe and Svetlana were assessing the soldiers as they approached. I could tell the girls were trying to determine if they could take them all out. Zoe was accomplished at fighting, and from what little I had seen of Svetlana, I knew she was even better, but the two of them seemed to realize that there was no way they could handle twelve armed soldiers at once. If Erica and Catherine had been conscious, the odds would have been different, but at the moment, we were outmanned.

The soldiers swarmed around us. They each looked like they felt embarrassed about doing this, but still, they were in the military and operating under orders, so they had little choice.

Alexander appeared upset as well. "I'm terribly sorry," he told us.

"There's no need to apologize to them," Cyrus snapped. "Tomorrow, they'll be thanking us for what we're doing." He looked at me, Mike, Zoe, and Svetlana. "Trust me, you'll soon see that this was the right decision."

But it wasn't. And I knew it.

Cyrus might have been protecting us in the short term, but he had condemned the earth to disaster.

Doomsday was coming.

FAMILY ISSUES

Tuckernuck Military Refueling Depot

Kotzebue, Alaska

July 19

0700 hours

"I guess you're not the only one whose grand-father is a lunatic," Erica told Svetlana with a sigh.

Despite Cyrus's insistence that we be locked up, Tuckernuck didn't have a prison, or any sort of holding cell at all. The closest thing to a crime that had ever occurred there was when a porcupine had got into the mess hall and eaten all the Doritos. The town of Kotzebue only had a small jail cell at their police station, and it happened to be full, holding four fishermen who'd been arrested the previous night for public inebriation and urinating on city hall. So the soldiers had locked us up in their bunkhouse instead—after impounding all our weapons and utility belts. Since the locks on the doors and windows were flimsy, the soldiers were also patrolling the perimeter to make sure that we didn't escape.

And escape was absolutely on our minds.

With every second that we were locked up, we were losing precious time to stop Ivan's doomsday plot. Mike, Zoe, and Svetlana had been trying to break into the soldier's footlockers to see if there was anything we could use as a weapon, while I had been trying to rouse Erica and Catherine from their sedative-induced slumber.

Catherine seemed to have received the stronger dose. I had managed to help her regain consciousness by waving dirty sweat socks under her nose, but she was still in a dream state, drowsily murmuring nonsense. The very first thing she'd said to me was, "I think I left my bassoon in Oxford. Could you go get it for me?"

Erica had regained her mental facilities faster, although the rest of her body remained stubbornly asleep. At the moment, she couldn't move anything but the pinky finger of her left hand. Meanwhile, sedatives tended to affect Erica's normal penchant for keeping things to herself. She was much more likely to open up emotionally under the effects of them, which she was doing now. "I mean, look at me," she told Svetlana. "My grandfather sedated me and locked me up. That's the kind of stuff that evil stepmothers do in fairy tales."

"Your grandfather is only trying to protect you," Svetlana said, jabbing a hairpin into the hasp of a footlocker. "Because *my* grandfather is the true lunatic. He is going to destroy the world!"

Erica twitched her pinky. "If my grandfather was only interested in protecting me, there were better ways for him to go about it. This was about control. He wants us to respect him as the leader of this mission, but he's repeatedly made mistakes. He allowed himself to get captured right off the bat, forcing us to come rescue him; he let Murray Hill knock us out and steal our helicopter—"

"Well, technically, that's on *all* of us," I said.

"Yes, but you're still a trainee," Erica pointed out. "Cyrus was the mission leader. It's his job to see that sort of thing coming. Then he was in such a hurry to tell Ivan about Operation Hornswoggle that he walked us right into an ambush. And he would have drowned if Mike hadn't rescued him. . . ."

"Which he didn't even say 'thank you' for," Mike grumbled. "Instead, he got testy with me."

"Of course," Erica said. "Because his pride was wounded. Cyrus knows he's losing his edge—and more importantly, he's worried that *we* know that too. So he's exerting his power where he can. Like making us sit on the sidelines while Doomsday goes off."

"Well, let's see if we can get back in the game." Zoe finished undoing the lock on a footlocker and dramatically flipped it open—only to frown with disgust at what lay inside. "Dang it. There's nothing in here but clothes and paperback romance novels. Not a single thing we can use as a weapon."

"Who here wants to make snickerdoodle cookies?" Catherine asked sleepily. "They're scrum-diddly-umptious!"

Svetlana continued fiddling with the footlocker she was trying to break into. "Your grandfather still seems to care about you," she told Erica. "All Ivan wanted to do with me was turn me into a miniature version of him."

"That sounds like Cyrus too," Erica observed sadly. "You know where he took me for my third birthday? An escape room."

"That doesn't sound so bad," Mike said.

"He didn't do it with me," Erica explained. "He locked me inside. By myself. And told me that if I couldn't get out within an hour that I was a shame to the family."

"Yikes," I said. "Did you solve it?"

"Of course I did," Erica said. "In fact, I broke the record for the fastest escape. But I'd told Cyrus that I wanted to go to the zoo. I wanted to see the giant pandas. He told me that the zoo was a waste of time and made me train instead."

"You think that was rough?" Svetlana asked. "You just saw the Icebox. That's where my grandfather brought me every summer. Instead of going to camp and getting to spend time with children my own age, I had to train with soldiers in that godforsaken place."

Erica realized she now had enough control over her arms to prop herself up on an elbow. "Cyrus started training me for hand-to-hand combat the day I could walk."

"Ivan started training me for combat *before* that," Svetlana countered. "His first gift to me as a baby was a rattle that had a stiletto hidden inside it."

"Cyrus taught me how to make my own cyanide when I was five."

"When I was that age, Ivan actually *poisoned* me. He put tiny amounts of arsenic in my porridge to help me build up resistance to it."

"Arsenic? That's nothing. Cyrus used to throw knives at me to test my reflexes."

"Only knives? You were lucky. Ivan once sent me out to face a grizzly with only a wooden spoon."

"I think this is a tie," Mike announced. "Both of your grandfathers stink."

Erica frowned at that. "I wouldn't go quite that far. I

mean, Cyrus did things his own way, but he still cares about me."

"Yes, I think Ivan cares for me too. Ah!" Svetlana finally jimmied the lock on the footlocker and lifted the lid.

Zoe scooted to her side. "Anything we can weaponize in here?"

"There's some aftershave," Svetlana noted. "That's flammable."

"That's a start." Erica was gaining more control over her body. She shifted into a sitting position.

Her mother was still loopy, though. "Goodness gracious," she murmured. "Someone's poisoned the salmon mousse!"

"What's the plan, exactly?" I asked Erica.

"We create a small incendiary device with the aftershave and set the bunk beds on fire. When the soldiers come in to see what's going on, we get the jump on them. Then, I fly us to the Arctic National Wildlife Refuge in the helicopter—"

"I don't want to be a downer here," Mike interrupted, "but the last time you flew us in a helicopter, we nearly died."

"That was a beat-up old trainer," Erica said dismissively.

"Which you were flying because you're only training to be a helicopter pilot," Mike reminded her. "Do you actually know how to fly the Sea Knight?"

"How hard could it be?" Erica asked.

"Um . . . *very* hard, I'm sure," Mike answered.

"It can't be that difficult," Erica claimed. "My father can do it."

Zoe said, "Your father might be a lousy spy, but he's a good pilot. I don't know if we can do this without him."

"Well we have to," Erica insisted. "He's already told us he's not going. So it looks like I'll have to fly the chopper."

"You can't even move your legs yet!" Svetlana exclaimed.

"I'm sure the feeling will come back eventually," Erica told her.

"Erica," I said, "You're still half-sedated. Your mother is completely zonked out. We don't have anyone who knows how to fly that helicopter, and we've got less than five hours to find the doomsday device somewhere in the Arctic National Wildlife Refuge and then dismantle it. I'm not sure we can pull this off."

Erica glared at me. "You're quitting now too? Just like my grandfather wanted us to do?"

I shrugged. "I'm not happy about it. But the odds are really stacked against us. I'm not sure we can even get airborne, let alone defeat Ivan."

Erica looked to the others. "What do all of you think?"

"I think Ben might be right," Mike said sadly.

"No one knows the odds better than him," Zoe added.

"I agree with Zoe's analysis of Ben's analysis," Svetlana put in.

"I think there's a peanut in my ear," Catherine stated.

"Well I'm not going to just sit here and do nothing." Erica got to her feet—and then toppled right back onto the bed because she still barely had any feeling in her legs. And since she didn't have much control over her arms yet either, she belly flopped onto the thin mattress and ended up with her face embedded in a pillow. "Dang it," she muttered.

There was a sudden yelp of surprise outside the bunkhouse, followed by the sound of someone collapsing.

Then we heard a key rattling in the door.

We all went on the alert, grabbing whatever we could find close at hand to use as weapons. There wasn't much to choose from. Svetlana grabbed the aftershave. Zoe grabbed some romance novels. Mike and I grabbed pillows.

Erica didn't grab anything, as she was struggling to sit up again.

A second later, Alexander barged in, looking furtive and worried. "If you want to stop Ivan," he whispered, "we have to go *now*."

All of us looked at him, confused. Erica finally managed to lift her head out of the pillows. "I thought you said this was a suicide mission."

"That was just to get my father to drop his guard," Alexander said, then thought to ask. "Er . . . is it a suicide mission?"

"Maybe not anymore," I replied. The odds had just shifted slightly in our favor. "Where's Cyrus?"

"I spiked his coffee with laxatives to put him out of commission," Alexander reported. "He'll be in the bathroom for a while. Then I took out the soldiers patrolling the bunkhouse with Dad's sedation gun. I figure we might have three minutes before the others realize something's wrong. So? Are you coming?"

Everyone turned to me.

"Now that we have someone who can fly the helicopter, this might just work," I said.

"Then let's get moving!" Mike declared.

Alexander raced to the bunk where Catherine was lying and hoisted her onto his shoulder.

"Whee!" she yelled. "Piggyback rides for everyone!"

Mike helped me lift Erica to her feet. She hooked an arm over each of our shoulders and let us drag her to the door.

Zoe and Svetlana joined us as we all hustled out of the bunkhouse and onto the tarmac.

Two soldiers were sprawled unconscious by the front door. There was also an unconscious goose nearby.

"Why did you knock out the bird?" Svetlana asked Alexander.

"Er . . . that wasn't quite on purpose," he confessed. "I had a little trouble aiming the sedation gun."

Sure enough, there were several sedation darts jammed into the walls of the bunkhouse. Alexander had obviously missed his targets a few times before finally striking them.

I plucked one of the darts from the doorjamb while Zoe and Svetlana relieved the unconscious guards of their guns.

The other Quonset hut was several yards away, and yet, we could still hear the distinct sounds of Cyrus in the bathroom there, dealing with the effects of his laxative. It sounded like an elephant walking through a room full of whoopee cushions.

We hustled across the tarmac to where the Sea Knight was parked.

"Dad," Erica said. "Why didn't you just side with us in the first place, when Grandpa first turned the soldiers on us?"

"We were outnumbered," Alexander replied. "And you know how my father gets when he's convinced he's right about something. If I'd revealed that I agreed with you, he would have sedated me, too. I wasn't happy about pretending to agree with him, but it was the only way I could engineer this."

Erica grimaced. "I'm sorry that I got angry at you earlier. I didn't realize you were conning Grandpa. That was some good acting. And good plotting."

Alexander blushed, embarrassed. "Thanks, sweetheart."

"You're my hero," Catherine cooed. "Although you smell like dead fish."

"It's been a long day," Alexander reminded her.

We reached the Sea Knight. Alexander opened the doors, and we all climbed in. He laid Catherine across a few jump seats, scampered into the cockpit, and started up the engines.

The sound immediately alerted the remaining soldiers at Tuckernuck that we were escaping. Within seconds, they raced out of the mess hall.

But by that point, we had already secured the doors, and the Sea Knight was lifting into the air. The soldiers could only stare up at us impotently as we rose above them.

Then Cyrus exited the Quonset hut as well, having rushed out of the bathroom so quickly that he was still zipping his pants. He shook a fist the helicopter and yelled something that we couldn't possibly hear, but which was certainly very angry.

Alexander angled northeast across Kotzebue Bay, heading in the general direction of the Arctic National Wildlife Refuge.

But while we had managed to overcome one hurdle, there were still many more ahead.

"All right," Mike said. "We may have lost some valuable time, but now, all we have to do is track down the doomsday device before Ivan can set it off. That shouldn't be too hard. I mean, how big is the Arctic National Wildlife Refuge?"

"Slightly over thirty thousand square miles," Erica informed him.

"What?!" Mike was so stunned, he had to lean against the side of the helicopter for support. "That's absolutely enormous!"

"Yes. It's the largest wildlife refuge on earth," Erica said.

Mike had gone pale with shock. "I thought wildlife refuges were like, thirty acres, maximum. There's one near my parents' house that only has twelve trees and a duck pond."

"Well this one's twice the size of Switzerland," Erica declared.

"Two Switzerlands?" Mike goggled at the thought. "There are only seven of us! How are we supposed to find this doomsday device in an area that big—let alone destroy it?"

"I don't think we can," I said.

The others turned to me, surprised.

"Then why did you say this mission might work?" Zoe demanded.

"I have a plan," I said. It had come to me in the bunkhouse, while listening to Erica and Svetlana discussing their grandfathers. I looked to Svetlana now. She was sitting beside Zoe and staring at me intently. "But I'm afraid it involves a very big risk for you."

"Whatever it is," Svetlana replied, "I'm in."

TRACKING

Arctic National Wildlife Refuge

Somewhere along the Beaufort Sea

July 19

1145 hours

The arctic plain along the northern coast of Alaska is larger than the entire state of California—and yet, there isn't a single tree in it.

The climate is too harsh and cold for trees to survive. Although, not too far to the south, there were millions of trees. Our path to the Arctic National Wildlife Refuge took us directly over the Gates of the Arctic National Park, which is home to the largest intact forest remaining in the United States. The pristine landscape below us was filled with jagged mountains, serpentine rivers, and boreal forests stretching for as far as the eye could see.

I heard it was staggeringly beautiful. But I slept through it.

Even though I was terribly nervous about Ivan Shumovsky's doomsday plan, I was also exhausted. There were a thousand other things I would have liked to have been doing with what might have been my final hours on earth, but I needed to be fully rested when the time for action came. So after laying out my plan—and getting everyone's agreement that it was probably our best shot—I took a nap.

I was so tired that, even in the loud, juddering helicopter, I passed out right away. I slept soundly for several hours, until Erica shook me awake and announced that we had arrived at the Arctic National Wildlife Refuge. I was farther north than I had ever been in my life—and, for that matter, farther north than almost any humans ever ventured.

The landscape below us, devoid of trees, was mostly rolling plains of tundra—and caribou. There were thousands of them, in herds so thick that it looked as though part of the refuge was carpeted. A few smaller herds of musk ox roamed among them; with their big, shaggy bodies, they looked like walking toupees.

There were also lots of mosquitoes.

We couldn't see them from the helicopter, of course, but the moment we landed, they descended upon us in great clouds, as though they were all bored of sucking the blood out of caribou and were eager to try some humans. The Sea Knight had come equipped with several gallons of insect repellent, but even after dousing ourselves with it, it wasn't completely effective.

I had never encountered tundra before. From the air, it had looked like a gigantic lawn, but the ground turned out to be covered with several inches of small, springy shrubs, rather than grass. Walking on it felt like crossing the world's largest kitchen sponge.

My plan involved splitting the team up. Svetlana, Zoe, Mike, and Catherine were going to stay in the refuge. Alexander, Erica, and I were only on the ground with them for less than three minutes. We quickly made sure that they had everything they needed to survive for a few days—just in case something went wrong, and we didn't get back. Then I took a few photos of them, and we said some hasty good-byes.

Mike and Zoe hugged me at once. There wasn't even time for them to do it separately.

"You've been the best friends I could ever ask for," I told them.

"Don't use past tense like that," Mike said. "You're gonna see us again."

"I know you can do this," Zoe added.

Although, in their eyes, I could see that both of them feared this might not be true.

Meanwhile, Catherine was hugging Erica. Alexander was still in the cockpit of the Sea Knight. He hadn't bothered to shut the helicopter down to save time taking off again.

"I love you," Catherine told Erica.

"I love you too, Mom," Erica replied, then reluctantly pulled away.

She and I raced back into the helicopter and then lifted off. Below us, Zoe and Svetlana held hands, while Catherine tearfully waved good-bye, and Mike swatted at mosquitoes. I kept my eyes locked on them as they shrank to tiny dots, lost in a sea of caribou.

Then Alexander headed for the northern coast so I could get to work on my part of the plan:

I had to find the Russian submarine.

We knew that it was heading toward us so that it would be close enough for its short-range missile to trigger the doomsday device. We also knew the submarine would need to surface in order to do that. The trick was, we had to find the sub in the brief window after it surfaced but before it launched the missile—which might only be thirty seconds long. And there were hundreds of square miles of ocean to find it in.

Since I was very good at math, it fell upon me to narrow our search area as much as possible.

Erica had downloaded the specs for the submarine, including how fast it could travel at top speed. And we knew exactly where the submarine had been at 1945 hours the day before, because we had watched it submerge after trying to blow us up. The Sea Knight had a trove of maps aboard, including many detailed ones of the northern coast of Alaska. Using all that information, I did my best to calculate where the sub would surface.

Unfortunately, there were still factors that I couldn't account for. I didn't know exactly how close Ivan needed to be to launch the missile, or if he had run into any strong currents on the way that had slowed him down, so the best I could give us was a rough estimate, which still left a very large amount of the Beaufort Sea that we had to patrol.

We did the best we could.

The one advantage we had was the ice.

Even in mid-July, the Beaufort Sea was covered with it. According to our maps, some of the ice would melt in late summer, but the breakup had only just begun. While the Chukchi Sea, where we had met Ivan before, was mostly open ocean with the occasional ice floe, the Beaufort was the reverse: a huge sheet of ice with only the occasional pocket of blue water. The ice stretched as far as we could see; it looked as though the entire earth had been coated with vanilla frosting.

In theory, when the submarine broke through the ice, the black conning tower would stand out against the stark white background. But until that happened, we had a huge area to monitor.

Alexander circled the section of the sea where I had calculated the submarine would appear, while Erica and I desperately searched the ice with binoculars. If the fate of the world hadn't been hanging in the balance, it might have been a lovely day. I spotted numerous polar bears, out roaming the sea ice for seals, and in the blue pockets of water, pods of beluga whales and narwhals emerged, spouting puffs of mist into the air.

As the clock ticked toward noon, we put the second part of our plan into action.

Svetlana had given us her phone, so that we could contact Ivan. Ideally, I would have let her make the call, but the Arctic National Wildlife Refuge was so remote that phone service was nonexistent. It was better along the coast, because the oil refineries arrayed there demanded it, but the coverage was still spotty at best.

Svetlana's phone was a Russian brand called a TectaFon, which Svetlana had admitted used technology stolen from western companies—and yet, it still didn't work that well. I brought up Ivan's number and started calling it.

The first call went directly to his voicemail. I immediately hung up and tried again. The next call did the same. And the next.

I started to get worried.

I had known that calling Ivan was a dicey move. There were a few reasons it might not work:

1. The cell service was too bad.

2. I had completely miscalculated where the sub might be, and it was well out of range.

3. Ivan was really, really angry at Svetlana for betraying him and didn't want to take her calls.

4. If Ivan was anything like my grandfather or Cyrus, then he couldn't operate his phone that well. He might have accidentally turned the ringer off—or dropped it into the toilet. (My grandfather did both of these things on a regular basis. Once he'd even managed to flush the toilet after dropping the phone in it.)

But my plan relied on making contact, so I kept trying.

The calls kept going to voicemail.

It was now one minute until noon.

"There!" Erica exclaimed, pointing out the window.

In the distance, the submarine's conning tower was erupting through the ice, creating a shower of frozen particles that glittered in the air. It was easily more than a mile away; only someone with Erica's exceptional sense of sight would have noticed it.

I had calculated correctly after all.

"I see him!" Alexander exclaimed, and banked the helicopter in that direction.

I dialed Ivan again, but the call went to voicemail once more.

"If we have reception now, then Ivan ought to have it too," Erica concluded. "He's ghosting Svetlana. Go to Plan B."

Plan B involved texting a photo to Ivan and hoping that he wasn't too busy unleashing doomsday to see it.

If he was, then we had to go to Plan C, which I didn't like at all.

Plan C meant intercepting Ivan's missile with our helicopter. Which would definitely make this a suicide mission.

I texted the photo.

Only, I had forgotten that, with our erratic cell reception and Svetlana's crummy phone, texting a photo might not happen as rapidly as I'd hoped.

Her phone slowly began to upload the photo.

We raced across the sea toward the submarine.

More of it had broken through the ice. The length of the entire craft was now visible—as was the artillery launcher that emerged from the hull.

The launcher swiveled in the direction of the Arctic National Wildlife Refuge.

The photograph still hadn't completely uploaded.

Alexander brought us in low. The great expanse of ice flashed by beneath us, gleaming in the summer sun.

I wondered if that would be the last thing I ever saw.

Erica grabbed my hand and squeezed it.

The photo finally finished uploading.

There was a soft whoosh as our text was sent.

Three seconds passed. Each felt like a century.

And then Svetlana's phone began to ring.

I handed it to Erica, since she spoke Russian better than me. She answered the phone.

"Svetlana?" Ivan asked. "Where are you?" I had learned enough Russian to understand him—but even if I hadn't been able to, the worry in his voice would have still been obvious.

"That photo should make it clear where Svetlana is," Erica told him. "She gave me her phone so that I could talk some sense into you. Call off Doomsday."

Ivan didn't respond for a few seconds.

We were almost at the submarine. The artillery launcher finished rotating and locked into place.

Alexander brought the helicopter to a stop in midair. We hovered between the submarine and its target, ready to sacrifice ourselves.

Finally, Ivan said, "How do I know you're not bluffing?"

"I can prove it," Erica replied. "Let's talk."

Another long pause followed. And then Ivan said, "Okay."

CONFRONTATION

Somewhere in the Beaufort Sea

July 19

1200 hours

Alexander set the Sea Knight down close to the submarine, and we stepped out onto the frozen surface of the sea.

I thought I had been cold before. I was wrong.

Even though I had several layers of clothes on, it felt as though I had just been thrown into a meat locker naked. The cold instantly seeped into my body. Within seconds, my fingers and toes went numb. Meanwhile, a frigid wind chilled us even further, as well as pelting us with thousands of tiny shards of ice. It was like being in the world's coldest sandblaster. The whole experience was miserable.

Although being inside the submarine was even worse.

After patting us down to make sure we weren't carrying any weapons, Ivan's men forced us into the sub at gunpoint. We descended through a hatch into the central control room, where the periscope, the steering mechanisms, and the launching system for the missile all were. The room was cramped and claustrophobic—but it turned out to be spacious compared to the rest of the submarine.

The Russians herded us into a passage that ran along the port side of the sub. It was so tight and narrow that even I had to hunch to get through it, and it passed a series of rooms that weren't much bigger than closets. There is no wasted space on a submarine. Every single inch is filled. There was so little room for the crew to move about that a third of them were confined to their bunks at any time—and now we had just added three more people. Metal flanges and bolts stuck out everywhere, waiting for an unsuspecting passerby to clock their head. The heating system was barely working, so it was almost as cold inside the sub as it had been outside. Worst of all, there was no ventilation. The air was stale and reeked of burnt fuel, body odor, bad breath, backed-up toilets, and the gas of forty men who'd been subsisting on canned borscht. And as if that wasn't bad enough, many of the Russian sailors were actually smoking cigarettes. After being in the fresh, bracing air above, it felt as though we had descended into a sewer.

Every twenty feet there was a bulkhead, a steel wall that spanned the submarine from side to side. Each of these had an oval steel door built into it, with a locking mechanism that looked like it belonged on a bank vault.

Erica noticed me looking at them curiously and explained, "The bulkheads are here so that, if one section of the sub springs a leak, it can be sealed off from the rest of the sub. Then the entire sub won't flood; only part of it will."

"Ah," I said, unsure whether to feel better knowing that the submarine had such safety systems in place—or to feel worse because I was on a craft that needed such safety systems at all. But now that I knew what they were for, the odd design of the bulkhead doors made sense. It was easier to build a perfect seal around a rounded oval door than a rectangular door with corners, although the oval shape meant that you couldn't just walk through each doorway; you had to maneuver through it. There was a raised steel portion at the bottom that you had to step over and another portion at the top that you had to avoid whacking your head on.

Finally, we reached the officers' mess, where Ivan sat, waiting for us. This was the nicest room on the ship, and yet it was still worse than many prison cells I had seen. It was only as long and wide as a twin bed, with a rickety table surrounded by bench seats. Since storage was in short supply on the sub, sacks of potatoes and cans of borscht were stacked all around, leaving very little room to maneuver. We wedged ourselves around the table like sardines.

Ivan's biggest thug remained in the doorway that led to the rest of the sub, glowering at us menacingly. The doorway was quite small, and the man was quite large, so he almost filled the entire space.

Ivan didn't bother with any pleasantries, like saying hello or offering us a nice cup of tea. Instead, he smacked his phone down on the table in front of us and demanded in English, "Explain this."

His screen was displaying the photograph I had texted him from Svetlana's phone.

I had taken the photo myself. Svetlana stood on the tundra in the middle of the Arctic National Wildlife Refuge. A large herd of caribou could be seen behind her. Zoe was by Svetlana's side, with a supportive arm around her.

"Isn't it obvious?" Erica began. "Svetlana is—"

"I'm not asking *you* to explain," Ivan interrupted, then looked to me. "I want *you* to explain. You are not a descendant of Cyrus Hale. Cyrus Hale is a lying, cheating weasel. I don't trust anyone in his family."

"Oh," I said uncomfortably. I had really been hoping that Erica would be allowed to do all the talking. "Er, well . . .

Svetlana is in the Arctic National Wildlife Refuge right now. So . . . if you blow it up, then you will also kill *her*."

Ivan looked as though he was wavering between concern and disbelief. "And how did you even know to be here now?"

"Svetlana took us to the Icebox," I replied. "She showed us how to sneak in through the emergency exit tunnel, how to break into your safe, how to steal your journal—"

"That is not possible!" Ivan interrupted.

"It is," I told him. "We did it."

"And all of you got out alive?"

"Yes. Although your flamethrower did burn off most of Cyrus's hair. Then Svetlana helped us decode your journal—and here we are."

Ivan scowled, obviously upset about hearing this new information. Then he looked back at his phone and scrutinized the photo carefully. "You expect me to believe that you just left my granddaughter out there in the wilderness with this one other girl?"

"They're not by themselves," I said. "We also left Erica's mother and my friend Mike with them. And Erica's mother is armed, in case of polar bears. Or grizzlies."

"But she is not in the picture," Ivan declared.

"No. I did take some others, though." I picked up Svetlana's phone to display them. "I had to choose the one that was best to text to you. The others weren't as good. See?

Svetlana's eyes are closed in this one. And Zoe's hair is in her face here. And in this one, I got part of my thumb in the photo. . . ."

"You're rambling," Erica told me.

"Sorry," I said. "I'm very nervous."

Ivan looked through the photos on Svetlana's phone, then returned to the single image I had texted him of Svetlana and Zoe. "This could still be a lie. How do I know Svetlana is not in some other part of Alaska?"

"We *did* think about that," I explained. "If we could have taken a photo in front of a big 'Welcome to the Arctic National Wildlife Refuge' sign, we would have—but it turns out that there isn't one of those. They don't even have a visitor center up there. But they *do* have tremendously large herds of caribou, so we left Svetlana by one of those."

"There are caribou in other parts of Alaska," Ivan declared.

"Yes, but this herd is *huge*."

"That's still not proof that she's in the ANWR."

"Well then, I suppose the best I can offer is: You know Svetlana. If she thought what you were doing was wrong, where do *you* think she would be right now to stop you?"

Ivan considered that for a while, then heaved an enormous sigh. "My granddaughter can be as stubborn as a musk ox."

"Ah," I said, then had to ask, "Are musk ox stubborn?"

"Don't you know anything about musk ox?"

"Er . . . no. I honestly didn't even know they existed until I saw one, like, half an hour ago."

"Well they are very stubborn. Just like Svetlana." Ivan gave us all a nasty look. "But she was never insubordinate. Until now. She was my little agent-in-training, willing to do whatever it took to please me. And then she meets you, and all of a sudden, she is nothing but trouble. She betrays me, prevents me from killing you, breaks into my fortress, decodes my secret plans—and now she attempts to thwart Doomsday. . . ."

"Sorry to interrupt," Alexander said meekly. "But did you just say 'attempts to thwart'? She hasn't thwarted it?"

"I have been working on these plans for decades!" Ivan proclaimed. "The United States must be brought to its knees for the crimes it has committed against Russia! Do you think I'm going to back off now just because my granddaughter has stabbed me in the back and put her life at risk?"

"Yes," Alexander replied. "We were really hoping that would be the case."

"I know you're upset at Svetlana right now," I added quickly. "But if you launch this doomsday plan, she will die. Is revenge on the United States worth her life?"

"Sometimes, sacrifices must be made for the greater

good," Ivan said. Although I detected a slight quaver in his voice as he spoke. Like maybe he was trying to convince himself that this was the truth.

I grabbed his phone back from him and enlarged the photo of Svetlana, so that her face filled the entire screen, and her eyes appeared to be boring into mine. Then I held it out to Ivan once more. "Go through with this and you will never see her again."

"I know," Ivan said sadly.

"The United States didn't cheat Russia in the deal for Alaska," I said. "The Croatoan did. And we defeated the Croatoan a few months ago. We thwarted *their* plans—and got all the leaders arrested. So really, if anything, you should be thanking us, rather than attacking us."

Ivan broke his gaze from the photo of Svetlana and looked at me with surprise. "*You* defeated the Croatoan?"

"Yes. Along with our friends, although Erica and I handled everything at the end."

"Erica, I can understand doing this," Ivan said. "She is obviously very skilled. But you? You look like you couldn't open a jar of pickles."

"Looks can be deceiving," Erica told him. "Ben's as good as they come. He's the one who calculated how to find you just now. And thanks to him, the Croatoan is no longer a threat to anyone. If you want, I'm sure we can get the leader to admit to Operation Hornswoggle. And we could probably even arrange for you to meet with her in person. Assuming that you don't do anything stupid right now."

Ivan grunted in response. He stared at Svetlana's photo for a while, apparently torn between his determination to see his longtime plans through and suffering the consequences of what that would mean.

Finally, Alexander couldn't take the silence anymore. "I know I ought to be keeping my mouth shut," he said, "but as a father, I just have to say something. I can't imagine anything more devastating than losing Erica—or my other daughter, Trixie. There is nothing I wouldn't sacrifice to protect them. And even though we aren't on the same side, I know you're not a terrible person. I know that you could never live with yourself if you brought harm to Svetlana."

Ivan looked up from the photo and gave Alexander an icy stare, which I considered bad news. But then a tear trickled down his cheek. He nodded slowly. "You're a very wise man," he said.

"I am?" Alexander asked, genuinely startled.

"I can't go through with this," Ivan said. "You have outmaneuvered me. I don't know how you convinced Svetlana to switch sides, but . . . you're right. I cannot do anything to hurt her."

A surge of relief came over me. Under the table, Erica

gave my hand a squeeze, and I realized that she had been equally as nervous.

Ivan set the phone down and turned to the agent who was still lurking in the doorway. "Doomsday is cancelled," he said in Russian. "Do not fire the weapon."

The Russian nodded. And then he took out his gun and aimed it at Ivan.

"Ivan Ivanovich Shumovsky, you are under arrest for treason," he said. "The doomsday device will be detonated as planned."

MUTINY

Aboard the *Akyna*

Somewhere in the Beaufort Sea

July 19

1215 hours

The relief I was feeling evaporated and was immediately replaced with cold, stark fear.

Now, not only was Doomsday still moving forward, but we were trapped inside a Russian submarine at gunpoint.

Ivan appeared equally dismayed. He gave his agent a wounded look and asked, "Dmitri, how can you do this to me?"

"Because you are a rutabaga," Dmitri replied angrily. It is highly likely that I misunderstood him, because my Russian wasn't great at the best of times, and now I was on the edge of panic, so I was having trouble focusing. But it's also possible that "rutabaga" was a very nasty Russian insult. "For years, you have driven us to plan this doomsday attack. We have suffered greatly to be by your side. We have left our families behind and lived a miserable existence in Siberia. And now, when the time of our triumph has finally arrived, you back out? Just because you are afraid to make a sacrifice? You are a flabby credenza, and we will no longer take orders from you." He turned and shouted to the others in the submarine. "Prepare to fire the missile!"

Another voice responded from deep inside the sub. "Yes, sir! The countdown is starting again. The missile will launch in one minute!"

Dmitri then returned his attention to Ivan and grinned cruelly. "The day of glory we have worked toward for so long is finally here. You should be happy, Ivan. But instead, you look like a—"

That was as far as he got.

Until thirty seconds before, Ivan Shumovsky had been our enemy. But now he was the enemy of our enemy, which didn't quite make him our friend—but it at least meant that we were on the same side. And despite his age, Ivan was still a formidable agent.

During the brief moment that Dmitri had turned away to yell to his fellow agents, Ivan had slipped his arms underneath the rickety table we were seated at. Now he suddenly sprang to his feet, lifting the table off the floor and smashing it into Dmitri's chest. Dmitri stumbled backward, and before he could recover, Ivan had snapped off one of the table legs and coldcocked him with it.

Unfortunately, there were many more agents besides Dmitri in the submarine, along with dozens of sailors, and they all appeared to be pro-Doomsday. Two of them were standing in the narrow passageway just outside the officers' mess, waiting to attack.

Only, Ivan got the jump on them. Now that he had decided not to set off the doomsday device, he was determined to save his granddaughter, using a Russian style of martial arts known as the Moscow Madman. We didn't practice it at spy school, as it was far less fluid and graceful than many other forms of martial arts, but a skilled practitioner of it like Ivan could do a lot of damage. Ivan now used the confined space of the submarine to his advantage. In the narrow passages, only one person could attack at a time, and as I had noted, there were plenty of jutting fixtures to stumble over or bang one's head on. Within seconds, Ivan had unleashed a St. Petersburg Slam, driving one agent backward into the other, forcing both to whack their heads on a low-hanging pipe and collapse, unconscious.

Erica instantly joined the fray, grabbing the only things she could find to use as weapons—two cans of borscht—and putting them to use. She slipped out the door behind Ivan to meet an attack coming from the other direction, heaving both cans at oncoming sailors. There were two loud clonks, followed by the thuds of both men keeling over.

"I'll lead the way to the launch controls!" Ivan yelled to us. "You keep the missile from firing!"

I grabbed my own cans of borscht, just in case of trouble, and followed the others into the narrow passage. Thanks to the quick work of Ivan and Erica, there were now five large Russians sprawled unconscious on the floor. In the narrow passageway, I had no choice but to run right over their prone bodies.

The officers' mess was toward the front of the sub. Beyond it, in the bow, were the officers' quarters and the torpedo room, which—due to the lack of space on a submarine—was also a sleeping quarter for the crew. In the opposite direction, toward the stern, were the navigation room and then the central command center, where we had entered—and where the controls for the artillery system were.

Even though Ivan and Erica had worked swiftly, we still only had thirty seconds left to stop the missile from launching.

Ivan was leading the way to the command center, bulldozing aside anyone who tried to stop him, while Erica faced the bow, taking on anyone who attacked from that direction. I followed Ivan along with Alexander, who had armed himself with some potatoes.

In the navigation room, Ivan performed a textbook Irkutsk Whirling Dervish, taking out three attackers in a single blow, then incapacitated a fourth with a Nizhny Novgorod Nutcracker.

Behind us, Erica was using the ancient martial art of Nook-Bahn-San to fend off the Russians. I couldn't see what she was doing, but I could hear the series of thwacks, yelps, and cries of pain that indicated she was dealing with her opponents handily.

There were only ten seconds left until launch.

A Russian built like a brick wall blocked the bulkhead door that led into the command center, but Ivan didn't even hesitate. Instead, he lowered his head like a bull and charged, slamming into the Russian's chest hard enough to knock the wind out of him and plowing him backward over the two smaller sailors who were unfortunate enough to be standing behind him.

I followed them all into the control center. The captain of the sub was positioned at the periscope, while a scrawny young sailor stood at what were obviously the launch controls, his thumb poised above a large green button while he watched a timer tick down the last few seconds.

I was too far away to interfere with him directly, so I threw a can of borscht at him.

My calculations were spot on to deliver a pinpoint strike

to his forehead. Unfortunately, my aim wasn't quite as good. The can whistled past him and beaned the captain instead. The impact drove the captain's face into the periscope, which didn't fully knock him out but left him reeling.

The scrawny sailor *was* distracted, however. He looked up from the button, startled, just in time to see the second can of borscht coming at him.

I had thrown this one better, but now the sailor ducked out of the way, and it merely glanced off his head.

The sailor snapped back to his feet and gave me a taunting *you missed* look—which was when Alexander caught him full-force in the nose with a potato.

The sailor stumbled backward into a radar station, and I scrambled into his place at the control panel just as the timer reached zero.

Directly beside the big green button, there was a big red one. Since the sailor had been planning to push the green button to launch, I figured this was the standard "green means go; red means stop" system. I reached for the red button . . .

But before I could, the scrawny sailor grabbed me from behind and wrapped his arm around my neck, yanking me away from the controls while simultaneously choking me.

Since the control room was slightly less cramped than the rest of the submarine, Ivan had lost the advantage of fighting his attackers one at a time in a confined space. He was currently battling three men—and we could hear more Russians heading our way from the stern.

"Alexander! Shut the bulkhead!" Ivan yelled.

"Right!" Alexander raced to the bulkhead door that led to the stern and tried to slam it closed. Unfortunately, another Russian sailor was in the process of coming through it. He caught the door before it could lock and tried to shove it back open. Alexander braced himself on the other side, trying to push it closed.

At the same time, Erica ducked through the bulkhead at the bow end of the control room, pursued by more angry Russians. She grabbed a pipe that ran along the ceiling, hoisted herself up and performed a perfect Radiant Donkey Kick, sending the first attacker back through the bulkhead and causing a domino tumble of Russians. Then she dropped to the floor and, following Alexander's lead, slammed the bulkhead door shut and locked it.

I couldn't get back to the controls to push the red button. The scrawny sailor was still choking me. My vision was starting to blur, and I feared it would only be a matter of seconds before I passed out, freeing my opponent to set off Doomsday.

At this point, it finally occurred to me that I was carrying a sedation dart.

It was one of the ones that Alexander had used back at Tuckernuck, when trying to knock out the guards. I had plucked it out of the doorjamb and then forgotten all about it. It was in one of the dozens of pockets on my jacket, small enough that the Russians had missed it while frisking me for weapons earlier. Now I fished it out and jabbed it into the thigh of the scrawny sailor who was choking me.

The sedative didn't work fast enough to knock him out immediately, but the sharp dart was enough to make him howl in pain and release his grip on my neck a tiny bit, letting me breathe again.

I lifted my feet off the floor, braced them against the control panel, and shoved backward as powerfully as I could.

This was a very basic combat move known as Flailing in Desperation. I didn't really have a plan. All I knew was that the submarine was filled with hard metal objects, and so, if I shoved my assailant in any direction, he was bound to hit one of them. Meanwhile, his body would hopefully cushion me from the impact.

It worked.

We flew backward together, only to come to a sudden stop as we slammed into some control panel or another. The scrawny sailor howled once again and then crumpled to the floor, freeing me from his grasp.

But the captain of the submarine was now lurching toward the launch system.

In the center of the room, Ivan continued fighting

three men at once. He was doing impressively well—but his strength was flagging. One of the Russians attempted to take Ivan down with a swift kick to his nether regions, only to come in contact with Ivan's steel underwear. There was a loud clang, and then the attacker shrieked in pain and hobbled away, clutching his wounded toes.

Close by, Alexander was still struggling to shove the bulkhead door shut. On the opposite side of the room, Erica jammed a wrench between the wall and the handle of the door she had locked, preventing anyone on the other side from opening the door again.

I raced the captain back to the controls for the launch system.

The timer was still at zero, and a Russian phrase flashed beneath it that read either *Ready to fire* or *Gargle the eggplant*. The captain dove for the green button.

I hip-checked him at the last second, sending him stumbling back into the periscope once again. His head caromed off it, and he dropped to the floor. Then, before any other Russians could grab me, I pounded the red button.

Alarms immediately began wailing throughout the submarine. The timer reset to one minute.

Ivan and the three men he was fighting all paused in the midst of their battle and turned to me with fear in their eyes.

"What did you do?" Ivan demanded.

"I pushed the red button," I replied.

Ivan grew even more worried. "That's the self-destruct button, you fool!"

The Russians forgot all about fighting Ivan. They simply bolted for the ladder that led to the exit hatch.

"I didn't know!" I told Ivan, and then thought to ask, "Why would anyone even build a self-destruct button into a submarine?"

Ivan started to give me an answer but then seemed to realize he didn't have one. "It seemed like a good idea at the time," he said.

The timer was counting down to zero again.

The motives of everyone on the submarine had now changed. The Russians were no longer trying to get into the control room to attack us, and we were no longer trying to fend them off. Instead, all of us were now focused on escape. Alexander stopped trying to shove his bulkhead door shut. Erica removed the wrench that was jamming the door she had gone through so much trouble to close.

"What are you doing?" Ivan asked her, concerned.

"I'm not locking people inside a sub that's about to sink," she replied, and then hurried for the escape hatch.

Ivan, Alexander, and I followed her, although Ivan paused by the launch controls to point out a small yellow on/off switch. "That's how you turn off the launch system," he told me.

"It's not very well marked," I said defensively. "While the self-destruct button is right there in the middle of the panel. That's a major design flaw."

Russians burst through the bulkhead doors at each end of the room and raced for the exit hatch as well.

I clambered up the ladder behind Ivan and emerged onto the steel hull of the sub. The air outside was still painfully cold—and now it was sleeting—but it was wonderful compared to the foul, stale interior of the submarine.

Erica, Alexander, Ivan, and I raced across the sub, jumped onto the ice, and then fled across it toward the helicopter. The ice, once again, was an obstacle course, filled with jagged shards and potholes and slick, slippery surfaces that made running over it extremely difficult, but we did our best.

There were several other emergency hatches on the submarine. All of them had been opened, and Russians were streaming out of them like ants fleeing an anthill.

Most of them scattered across the ice, simply trying to get as far from the sub as they could before it self-destructed.

Although a few had the presence of mind to head for our helicopter, recognizing that it was the best way to escape.

"Don't let any of them get on board!" Ivan warned. "You can't trust them! I know—I trained them!" Even though he had just been through a nasty fight, he still ran across the ice with impressive speed.

Erica moved even faster, though. She had carried the helicopter keys herself this time, to ensure that Alexander didn't lose them. She made it to the Sea Knight well ahead of us and had the helicopter started up by the time the rest of us reached it.

It had been sixty seconds since I had initiated the self-destruct system.

A series of explosions detonated behind us.

I chanced a look back.

Huge balls of flame had erupted from several different points on the submarine, tearing holes in its flanks and sending bits of metal flying through the air.

It appeared that all the Russians had managed to evacuate safely. Most of them formed a ring on the ice a safe distance from the exploding sub, watching the fireworks.

Although three of them were directly behind me. One grabbed my jacket as I climbed into the helicopter and tried to pull me back out again, while the other two scrambled for the door.

Without even thinking about it, I fended off my attacker with a quick Silverback Elbow Jab, an Angry Yeti Throat Punch, and the Ordeal of a Thousand Smacks to the Face— although I was only ten slaps in before he scurried away in fear. Meanwhile, Ivan took out both the other Russians at once with a Volgograd Roundhouse so powerful that it sent the two of them skidding across the ice.

Alexander had already joined Erica in the cockpit. Before any more Russians could get to us, the helicopter lifted into the air.

More explosions rocked the submarine. The heat from the blasts was so intense, it overwhelmed the cold for a few seconds.

The scuttled sub quickly sank back through the ice. The dark arctic water enveloped it, and it went down for the last time.

Ivan stood in the open doorway of the Sea Knight, staring wistfully at the spot where the sub had been—and at all the Russians who, until only minutes before, had been his comrades.

"Don't worry about them," Erica said. Now that Alexander was at the controls, she had exited the cockpit. "We'll alert the navy, and they'll send a rescue boat. Your men will end up prisoners, but they'll live."

Ivan nodded sadly, then slid the door of the helicopter shut.

I strapped myself into a jump seat beside Erica.

Even though we had managed to thwart Ivan's doomsday plan, I couldn't fully relax. We had no way to contact Zoe, Mike, Catherine, and Svetlana to tell them of our success. It was a few minutes after the doomsday device would have detonated, so they certainly knew that we had delayed the attack—but I figured they were still nervous, expecting that something could go wrong at any minute. It wouldn't be until they saw us returning to get them that they'd finally feel safe for sure.

Below us, thousands of caribou grazed along the icy shore. Calving season had been only a few weeks before, so hundreds of youngsters were gamboling about playfully.

Erica watched them through her window, beaming. "Aren't they adorable? They have no idea how close they just came to being destroyed."

"Nope," I agreed. "You saved the day, as usual."

"*We* saved the day," Erica corrected, and then gave me a kiss on the cheek.

"Yuck," Ivan grumbled. He was sitting in the jump seat across from us, obviously miserable about how everything had gone. "It was such a good plan," he said sadly. "Now, it is ruined—and I am a traitor to my country."

"I'm sure the CIA will be happy to bring you aboard," Alexander said.

Ivan spat on the floor. "I will never work for the CIA. Cyrus Hale would be insufferable. He is probably waiting with Svetlana to mock me right now."

"Oh, Cyrus isn't with Svetlana," I told him.

Ivan looked to me curiously. "He is not on this mission?"

"No," I replied. "He wanted to let you go through with it. So we had to mutiny."

"And how did you do that?"

"Alexander gave him a whole bunch of laxatives."

For the first time since I had met Ivan, he laughed. A deep, hearty chortle. "You gave Cyrus the poops?"

"Yes," Erica said.

Ivan laughed even harder. "And you also said, when my booby trap flamethrower went off, it burned off all his hair?"

"Most of it," I replied.

Ivan was now laughing so hard that tears were streaming down his face. It was infectious. The thought of Cyrus with his hair singed off, along with my relief at having saved the day, overcame me. Before I knew it, I was laughing so hard that I was crying as well.

So was Alexander.

Even Erica, who wasn't prone to laughter, was giggling a bit.

"I guess some good came out of this day after all," Ivan wheezed between laughs.

"Yeah," Erica tittered. "I guess it did."

We raced onward over the herds of caribou, heading to reunite with our friends, laughing the entire way.

July 21

From: Special Agent Tina Cuevo, International Wildlife Anti-Smuggling
Task Force
To: Ben Ripley

Just wanted to give you an update on the search for your pal Murray.
A force from the local Army Reserve has spent the last three days
combing the area around the stolen helicopter. They found evidence
that Murray survived the wreck: footprints leading away from it, lots of
food wrappers—and a very soiled pair of underwear that he abandoned.
(Guess he was pretty scared during that crash landing.)

However, they didn't find Murray himself. I suppose it's possible that he
survived, but you and I both know that Murray has the survival skills of a
tuna sandwich, so I wouldn't bet on it. I'm figuring there's a much better
chance that he got eaten by a bear. There were a *lot* of bears around
that chopper wreckage. So. Many. Bears. I guess there was a lot of candy
in your supplies? And several cans of chocolate frosting? (How many
cupcakes are you making in that spy camp of yours?)

Anyhow, there's no sign of Murray. The closest towns (which really aren't
that close at all) have been notified to keep an eye out for him, but I'm
thinking that, if he hasn't shown up by now, we're not going to hear from
him anymore. This might sound callous, but I say good riddance. The guy
caused me plenty of trouble—although not nearly as much as he caused
you—and, frankly, even before he turned out to be evil, he was always
kind of a know-it-all jerk.

That said, if he does show up, I'll let you know ASAP.

Gotta go. Busting a huge iguana smuggling ring today.

Stay safe,

Tina

P.S. I hear you thwarted another plot to destroy the world, you lucky duck.
Nice work.

July 22

Hey—

I know you and I have had our differences in the past, but before you shred this letter, hear me out. I have gone through an awful lot of trouble to get it to you.

In fact, I've really had nothing but trouble since I last saw you. I've been incarcerated in the bunghole of the universe, with no one for company except thousands of walri. (And you know how I feel about walri.) Then I managed to escape, which was no picnic. I've been fighting my way through the wilderness for the past week, living off moss and earthworms, getting sucked dry by mosquitoes, trying not to get eaten by bears. But now I have made it back to civilization (or at least, what passes for civilization in rural Alaska), and I'm mad.

So why am I reaching out to you? Even though the last time we saw each other, you wanted to kill me? Because, simply put, we need each other. You don't sit by yourself on an island surrounded by walri for weeks on end without concocting an evil plan or two—and the one I've come up with is a doozy. But I need your help to pull it off.

Of course, I can't tell you what the plan is right now. This isn't the safest way to transmit information. But you should be expecting a visit from me soon. I'm letting you know now so you don't flip out when I show up and call security on me.

Trust me, you'll want to hear me out. Because this plan of mine will make both of us stinking RICH—and destroy Ben Ripley once and for all.

I'll see you soon,

You know who

acknowledgments

You will probably not be surprised to learn that this book was inspired by a trip to Alaska. About a year into the Covid pandemic, once vaccines had been developed and the world was beginning to open up again, my father and I headed to Kenai Fjords National Park. It is one of the most amazing places I have ever been, and from the moment I arrived, I knew it was the perfect starting point for an adventure. So, thank you to everyone on the staff at the Kenai Fjords Lodge (which is the only place you can stay in the park without camping and sits in the exact location where I set the new version of spy school). I am indebted to all of you for all the great things you took us to do, and for all the knowledge you shared with us (in particular, the history of Russia in the area, and its extreme reliance upon sea otter pelts).

One of the best things about travel is the friends you make while doing it. My father and I were lucky enough to go on a kayaking trip up to the Aialik Glacier with the Todd family: Alan and Perry and their children, Hattie and Robertson. We all hit it off tremendously while I was plotting the action sequence at the beginning of the book, and we have stayed friends since.

Once I had the story worked out, I felt I had to get back to Alaska. It is such an enormous state, it's hard to see more than a tiny sliver of it each time you go. I wanted to see walruses. And really big bears. This time, both my children joined me as we headed out to Wildman Lodge, which is possibly the most remote place I have ever stayed. The staff there was excellent—and educational—as well.

Back in the lower forty-eight states, I am so thankful to my ever-expanding group of close friends in the writing world: Rose Brock, Sarah Mlynowski, James Ponti, Julie Buxbaum, Max Brallier, Gordon Korman, Christina Soontornvat, Karina Yan Glaser, Julia DeVillers, Alyson Gerber, Jennifer E. Smith, Adele Griffin, Anna Carey, Leslie Margolis, Morgan Matson, and Maureen Goo.

Through writing, I have also been lucky enough to become friends with one of my favorite investigative journalists, A.J. Jacobs. I had been a fan of A.J.'s for years when one day I received an email from him saying that his kids were fans of mine. I learned all those cool facts about *Kryptos* at the CIA from A.J., who actually got to see it while doing research for his excellent book, *The Puzzler*. (If you like puzzles of any sort, that book is absolutely worth a read.) In addition, I learned from A.J. that, if you like someone's work, you might as well send them an email to let them know. They'll certainly appreciate it!

And speaking of appreciation, on the professional front, there are many wonderful people to thank at my publisher,

Simon & Schuster, as well: Krista Vitola, Leila Sales, Justin Chanda, Lucy Ruth Cummins, Erin Toller, Beth Parker, Roberta Stout, Kendra Levin, Alyza Liu, Anne Zafian, Lisa Moraleda, Jenica Nasworthy, Hilary Zarycky, Chava Wolin, Chrissy Noh, Ashley Mitchell, Brendon MacDonald, Amaris Mang, Nadia Almahdi, Christina Pecorale, Victor Iannone, Emily Hutton, Emily Ritter, Theresa Pang, and Michelle Leo.

Also, thanks to my intern, Lilian Liu, and to R.J. Bernocco and Mingo Reynolds at the Kelly Writers House at the University of Pennsylvania for continuing this great program. And finally, I couldn't get any of this done without my amazing assistant, Emma Chanen, who masterfully handles everything I ask of her.

On the home front, thanks (and much love) to my father, Ronald Gibbs, for coming along with me on that trip to Kenai, as well as to Jane Gibbs; Suzanne, Darragh, and Ciara Howard—and finally, Dashiell and Violet, my incredible kids. I'm not sure how many other children would be willing to go to the ends of the earth with their father because he felt that he needed to see some walruses up close, or who would hunker down in the tundra for a few hours to watch a mother bear the size of a standard sedan with her cubs. But my kids aren't just willing; they actually enjoy these trips and make them a delight. I am lucky to be their father.